W9-AYG-790

DAVID & DELLA

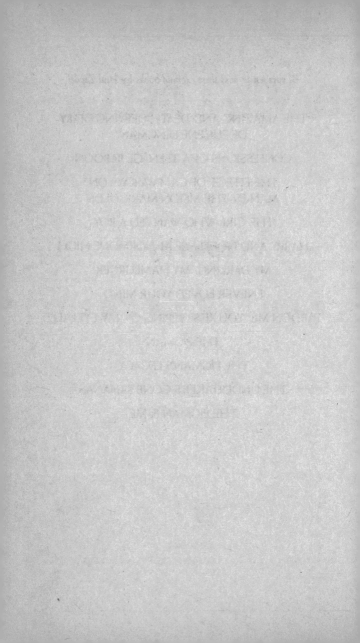

DAVID & DELLA

A novel by

PAUL ZINDEL

BANTAM BOOKS
NEW YORK · TORONTO · LONDON · SYDNEY · AUCKLAND

RL6.2, age 012 and up

DAVID & DELLA

A Bantam Book / December 1995

The Starfire logo is a registered trademark of Bantam Books, a division of
Bantam Doubleday Dell Publishing Group, Inc.
Registered in U.S. Patent and Trademark Office and elsewhere.

Reprinted by arrangement with HarperCollins Children's Books,
a division of HarperCollins Publishers.

ISBN 0-553-56727-6

Published simultaneously in the United States and Canada

Bantam Books are published by Bantam Books, a division of Bantam
Doubleday Dell Publishing Group, Inc. Its trademark, consisting of the
words "Bantam Books" and the portrayal of a rooster, is Registered in
U.S. Patent and Trademark Office and in other countries. Marca
Registrada. Bantam Books, 1540 Broadway, New York, New York 10036.

PRINTED IN THE UNITED STATES OF AMERICA

OPM   0 9 8 7 6 5 4 3 2

For Robert O. Warren

✦✦✦✦✦

1

✦✦✦✦✦

The most mind-boggling adventure of my
life started around six weeks ago on September 17th. That was the same day my
mother and father flew out of Kennedy Airport.
They had an assignment to write a magazine ar-
ticle about the success of McDonald's quarter-
pounders, Adidas sneakers, and Levi's button-fly
jeans in Budapest. I'd been used to them leaving
me alone at our apartment for years; besides,
this trip of my parents' sounded more boring
than usual.

Having no parents around is common at my
school, because most of them spend a lot of time
shopping at factory-outlet stores, hot-air bal-

looning, and taking How to Conduct Your Own Divorce courses at the Adult Learning Annex. And, hey, that's not a value judgment—that's just the way things are nowadays.

"You're sure you'll be all right, David?" Mom asked, heading for the door. She had gotten her hair bobbed for the trip, and wore a white sports jacket with large shoulder pads.

"He'll be fine!" my father said. He gave the few hairs he had left on his scalp a blast of hair spray a hurricane couldn't mess with.

"Remember, David, you didn't drive your girl-friend psycho," Mom said. "Kim had a lot of problems long before she met you. I heard she used to steal from Catholic Charities."

"She was always loony tunes," Dad said. "The druggist told me it was her parents who drove her crazy. He said they were both way over six feet tall, yelled at her too much, and bet on horses."

Mom hugged me. "And stop worrying about your writer's block! Before you know it, you'll forget all about that girl and write a lot more of those *different* stories you write."

"The one you wrote about the cannibal children who invite their math teacher for dinner was excellent," Dad said.

"Thanks."

The intercom buzzed.

"Taxi's here!" Mom shouted.

In a second they were dripping with luggage, their voices sputtering radio static.

"David, are you sure we left you enough money? . . . Take care of . . . David, I left all the telephone and fax numbers. . . . We love you. . . . Don't forget . . . Remember, you didn't drive poor Kim insane. She was nuts already!"

Finally, they were gone.

I'd have a month of peace. Maybe two, if I was lucky.

All this and it wasn't 7 A.M.

I'm the only boy I know of at George Washington High who helped drive his girlfriend insane. The girl was Kim Stark. She freaked out almost a year ago and tried to jump out of Mrs. Midgeley's third-floor honors biology class window. Kids in the class told me she yelled that she was going to shish kebab herself on the school flagpole. Now, of course, she's in a mental hospital somewhere in Illinois.

I toasted an English muffin in our G.E. toaster oven, smeared it with margarine, and sprinkled it with Equal and cinnamon. I made my usual decaffeinated cappuccino and went down the hallway to my room.

Kim's suicide attempt was one of the first things ever to shock me deep down in my gut. Before that the only things that bothered me were news reports on how a water buffalo in New Delhi was hanged for being a witch, or how a teenager in London was so shocked by winning a lottery that he went into a coma for three years. Well, maybe *one* other thing did bother me—I never had a really good pal or friendship that lasted very long.

A lot of people treat me like I'm some kind of weird event. I've been accused of being selfish, stoop-shouldered, self-centered, too smart for my own good, a dreamer, and a pizza freak—and those are only my parents' complaints. But they don't mean to be nagging, neurotic, and critical. It's just that they live busy lives traveling all around the world, scuba diving, eating exotic foods, and faxing. They can afford to be free-lance journalists because my mom's father left them some money when he kicked the bucket after working fifty-three years as a certified public accountant.

I want to be a professional writer too, but not like them. I like to write plays. Two years ago I won honorable mention in a teenage playwriting contest run by the American Cancer Society. I had seen a notice about the contest at school, and entered it because I wanted to win something just once in my life. I figured no other kid in his right mind would bother writing a play. I was wrong. I came in around eighty-seventh and was awarded a Parker ballpoint-pen-and-pencil set.

It had taken me an hour to write the play. I called it *The Miracle at Carnegie Hall*. It was about a teenage violinist who gets a brain tumor but recovers in time to play a symphonic arrangement of "Bridge Over Troubled Water."

The important thing was that I learned I liked to write plays. I wrote about daring topics: the struggle of two great Boy Scout pals to avoid having their necks bitten by a vampire camp counselor or the story of a high school dietician and her cafeteria workers who turn out to be alien lizards visiting earth to find new food sources. I wrote a play a month until the day my girlfriend tried to impale herself on the flagpole. Then something snapped. I couldn't write anymore. I was blocked.

What really changed my life on September 17th was not my parents' departure but what was waiting for me at school on the George Washington High bulletin board. There was a handwritten ad, scribbled on a three-by-five card, that said STUDENT THEATER COACH! ACTING LESSONS! DIRECTING! WRITING! CALL DELLA JONES, PHONE 555–4827. CHEAP!

Like most New York City schools, we've got thousands of kids flooding the place, which is one reason it's hard to make any really close, lasting friendships. Lots of the kids have professional experience in show business. There's always some kid from GW High showing up on a TV commercial pretending she loves eating Eggo frozen waffles or swilling a Diet Pepsi while bouncing on a trampoline. One talented, anorexic boy in the junior class got permission to tour Japan in *The Sound of Music, starring Debbie Boone.* Even the senior class advisor, Miss Feinberg, quit teaching last year to join The Big Apple Circus. But I had never heard of Della Jones before.

I used one of the student pay phones outside

the auditorium to dial the number. I was about to hang up after five rings when someone answered.

"Hello?" a very sophisticated voice said.

"Hi," I said. "I'd like to speak to Della Jones. I saw a notice on the school bulletin board."

"What school?"

"George Washington High."

"This is Della Jones. Who's this?"

"My name's David. David Mahooley."

"That's a good name for an actor."

"I'm not an actor. I write plays. That is, I used to write plays until my girlfriend tried to commit suicide. Maybe you heard about her, Kim Stark, the girl who tried to leap out of Bio 305 last year?"

"No. I don't go to George Washington. I put my ads up at a lot of schools."

"How old are you?"

"Sixteen."

"Me too. What school do you go to?"

"The Academy for Professional Children. But right now I'm in the middle of some unusual circumstances I don't feel like talking about on the phone."

"That's cool."

The more she spoke, the more she sounded like she was from England or one of those other countries that have girls who are both beautiful and know practical things like how to milk a cow. I started to talk nonstop about my heartbreak over Kim and my writer's block.

"Kim and I loved to play miniature golf and go see horror movies, and her mother left big, medium-rare roast beefs in the refrigerator for us to snack on, and . . ."

She cut me off. "Hey! I'm twenty dollars an hour. Do you want to make an appointment or not?"

"Yes."

"When?"

"Today."

"What time?"

"I get home from school by four. My folks are on a trip."

"Where do you live?"

My voice cracked. Someone was actually going to try to help me. "Thirty-two Lincoln Plaza. It's the high-rise between Sixty-second and Sixty-third on Broadway."

"What apartment?"

"Third floor, apartment 3D. Tell the doorman

you want David Mahooley."

"You're on," she said, and hung up.

◆◆◆◆◆

Take away love and our earth is a tomb.
— ROBERT BROWNING

Never eat more than you can lift.
— MISS PIGGY

◆◆◆◆◆

2

◆◆◆◆◆

I made it home by 3:23 and ran straight into the bathroom. I scrubbed my face with Clearasil facial wash, wet down my brown hair (especially the piece on top that stands up like a feather), and trimmed around my ears with the electric dog-grooming clipper I used to use on my dog, Rasputin, before he died last year of old age. He was just a mutt, but every time I use his clippers I miss the sloppy, wet kisses he'd give me whenever I came home from school. Rasputin was my best pal last year except for Daniel Barker. I used to be able to tell Daniel anything. We'd play catch in the park, see all the best horror movies, and we thought we were going to be pals forever. But his mother and father got into a really mean divorce, which drove Daniel so bananas, he punched a school-bus driver and got sent to a military prep school in Vancouver. They don't even let him write to me.

My bedroom has a sliding glass door that leads to a terrace. I used to find it inspirational to sit outside and watch the traffic three stories below and the busy entrance to our building. Now my sharpened pencils, Sony tape recorder, and Smith Corona Word Processing typewriter XD 7500 lay dead. The most alive doohickey in my room was a store dummy on a metal stand I had bought the week before at a flea market on Columbus Avenue. The mannequin's nose and chin were exactly like Kim's, but the rest of it looked more like a big voodoo doll. It was made of latex rubber that felt exactly like human skin. I knew I looked like a fool carrying a naked mannequin home on the Broadway bus during rush hour, but I was willing to try anything to start writing again.

At four P.M. the intercom buzzed.

"Joe? Joe?" I called down to the doorman.

"Yeah," Joe's voice crackled out of the speaker.

"David, you got Della Jones down here to see you. Want me to have one of the porters bring 'er up?"

"No!" I said. "Send her up by herself! By herself!"

I fired off several blasts of Lysol Country Scent air spray, straightened a large wall photo of my mother and father riding camels from their assignment at Club Med in Morocco, and did a last minute check of my front teeth for specks of Doritos and Cheese Doodles.

The door chimes sounded.

I looked out of the peephole of the front door. A pair of dark sunglasses stared back at me.

I started to open the door. Suddenly, it was shoved wide by a white cane swinging from side to side. I jumped out of the way as a girl plowed into the apartment tapping her cane like a machine gun.

"David Mahooley?" she screeched. "Is this David Mahooley's apartment? Hello in here?"

"You're the student theater coach?"

"Who'd you think I was?"

She swirled around in a long blue dress with shiny beads all over it. In her left hand she clutched a beat-up old gym bag.

"You sounded British on the phone."

"Yeah. Well, I'm basically an actress, you know," she said, flinging her great mass of hay-colored hair to the left side of her head. "I can sound Nipponese if I want to."

"*You're* Della Jones?"

"Yes!" she shrieked. She stopped banging her cane and took a deep breath. "You said on the phone that your parents took off on a trip?"

"I think there's been a mistake."

"Oh, there's no mistake, unless you lied."

"I don't lie."

"You writers are all so cute the way you call it *fiction*." Her head gyrated like a radar dish. "Where are we going to work?"

"I'm sorry, but you didn't tell me you were blind."

"How many jobs do you think I'd get saying I was a BLIND student theater coach? I told you. I'm in the middle of some rather unusual circumstances—one of them is being unsighted."

I was as thrown as when my corner newspaper stand has headlines like: GEORGIA TO OUTLAW TOAD LICKING and WOMAN DISCOVERS GOOEY CHUNKS IN HER BRAN MUFFIN ARE PIECES OF DEAD MOUSE.

I grabbed some cash from my pocket. "You said it was twenty dollars." I pressed the bill into her left hand. She dropped her gym bag and shoved the money into a waist pouch.

"Look," I said, "after I spoke to you I came home and got a lot of good writing ideas."

"Now you *are* lying."

"No."

"Look, Mahooley, I'm not an idiot. You said you wanted to write some kind of memorial play for your old main squeeze. Kim was her name, right?"

"Yes. . . ."

Her head was angled to my left so it looked like she was talking to the photo of my parents grinning on the camels. "You said you felt guilty, that you drove her to try to skewer herself?"

I put the gym bag back into her hand. "Look, I just don't need you today. Maybe some other time. I really enjoyed meeting you."

Suddenly, her body began to shudder. Tears rolled down from under her dark glasses. "Oh, God! You think I'm despicable."

"No I don't."

She swung her head so her mess of hair split to

straddle her face and dripped to her waist. "I was a great actress. I studied with Strasberg, Meisner, all the great acting teachers."

"I'm glad. . . ."

"Before my accident, everyone knew I would grow up to be another Glenn Close or Whoopi Goldberg! No kid in this city could act like me!" She went pale as she lowered herself into one of my mother's best living room chairs. "Quick, please, I'm going to pass out!"

"What's the matter?"

"I need a drink."

"I've got low-fat milk or orange juice."

"Something with alcohol in it!"

"I can't hand out my parents' liquor."

"Sure you can! Quick! What do they have?"

I rushed back to the hallway and opened the door to the liquor cabinet. "White wine," I called to her.

"Imported?"

"No."

"What do they have in red?"

"Gallo burgundy."

"Any gin?"

"Only Smirnoff's vodka."

"Great. No rocks, with a twist of lemon."

I grabbed the bottle and dashed to the kitchen. I poured a shot and cut a sliver from an old lemon I found in the refrigerator. I hurried back and carefully placed the drink in her hands. She clutched it and threw it back into her throat.

"It's not my fault I went blind," she said, chewing on the twist.

"Of course not." I stayed ready to catch her if she keeled over.

"The drunken husband of some TV-news anchorwoman jumped the barrier on the Sawmill River Parkway and slammed head-on into a car I was in. *I'm only sixteen years old and I'm blind!*"

"I'm sorry."

She wiped her mouth. "I went through the windshield, glass splinters the size of nails ripping into my eyes. I would have been a greater actress than Marilyn Monroe."

"Look, I said I was sorry."

"I still have more talent in my blood than any of them. I have so much to give and teach!"

"You can't help being blind."

She swung her cane, crashing it into my right foot. "Oh David, the moment I heard you on the phone, I knew you were a real loser."

"That's really the pot calling the kettle black, isn't it?" I was sorry the moment the words were out of my mouth.

"Look," she said, "I don't know how to sugar-coat this, but you are a real dork, aren't you? I mean, that's why you called me, right?"

I felt as helpless as one of those poor sacrificial goats they throw off the top of church towers at Madrid fiestas. Della Jones was blind, but it was as though she could see right through me.

"I know all about crumbled dreams!" she said. "In that department I wrote the book." She reached out. Her hand landed on my left knee. "Oh David, you *need* me to help you. Where do you write?"

"In my room."

She stood up and began tapping her cane forward. "Take me there. That's where we'll begin."

I picked up her gym bag, held her elbow, and guided her down the hallway.

"Don't worry," she said, "I'll unblock you. Today you'll begin to write again."

◆◆◆◆◆

A boy in love often mistakes a pimple for a dimple.
—JAPANESE PROVERB

♦♦♦♦♦

3

♦♦♦♦♦

ella was the first girl to be in my room since Kim.

"Have you helped a lot of writers?" I asked as I steered her over the threshold.

"I've coached plenty," she said, her cane swinging from one side to the other like a metronome.

"What do you do?"

"First I oil my students' necks."

"Oil their necks?"

"It's a basic technique to loosen tension. You'll see. Look, I know this'll sound freaky, but do you mind if I *feel* your room?"

"I don't mind."

She let go of my arm and started caning her way forward. "When I'm coaching someone, the things they have around them tell me a lot about their talent." She headed straight for a pile of dirty laundry I'd left on the floor. I scooted past her and shooed it out of her way. She turned suddenly and marched toward an open closet. I closed it so she wouldn't crash her head into the door. Next she was on a collision course with the mannequin. I lifted it and laid it on my bed out of the way.

Her cane smacked wood.

"What's this?"

"My bed."

"I can oil your neck while you're lying down."

"I wouldn't be comfortable. I'll sit in my desk chair."

"No problem."

"What kind of oil do you use?"

"Safflower, zero cholesterol."

"I don't like being touched unless I'm completely relaxed," I said.

"Madonna had me massage her neck twice a day when she was in New York recording her last album." Della reached her hands out to feel along the wall.

"You massaged Madonna's neck?"

"Sure. A lot of creative people know they write, sing, and do everything better with a massaged neck. The increased blood supply to your brain lets you live twenty years longer than those who don't do it."

"I never heard of that."

"It's a secret the United States government has to hide from the poor or they'd riot."

"What other famous people did you . . . coach?"

"Stephen King. Elton John. Joyce Carol Oates when she used to hang out with all those strange boxers. She's a very famous writer."

"You helped Joyce Carol Oates with a plot?"

"I don't gossip about clients. Are you relaxed yet?"

I sat down in the swivel chair at my desk. "No."

"Jeez! I should have brought my subliminal hypnotic *Ocean Waves* cassette to play." The fingers of her left hand reached out and found the aluminum handle to my terrace door. "What's this?"

"It leads out to my terrace."

She flung the door open. "Does it have a good view?"

"If I lean over the railing I can look left and see the bottom corner of one of the Metropolitan Opera's Chagalls."

"I feel a mist. Is there a fog?"

"No, I've got a neighbor on the terrace up across who's into hydroponics."

"What's hydroponics?"

"He grows giant vegetables in vats of water."

"Like what?"

"He's got cucumbers over five feet long."

Dogs began barking. "Why are those dogs making such a racket?"

"He's into hydroponics and raises mean, vicious, giant schnauzers. Say, how come you don't have a guide dog?"

She closed the terrace door. Her head turned so it looked like she was speaking to an Einstein poster above my TV. "I *had* one, but he got wounded last month in crossfire from a drug bust that went down near Zabar's delicatessen."

"That's awful."

"Oh, he'll live, but I won't get him back for a while yet."

She put her cane down. Her hands walked like tarantulas up the wall above my desk. "What's this?"

"That's my story clothesline. Whenever I get

an idea for a play I'm working on, I write a big note to myself with a Magic Marker and pin it up so I don't forget."

"That's so *different*."

"Thank you."

I was embarrassed as her fingers explored the nearly empty clothesline.

"How many plays have you written?"

"Seventeen."

"Were any of them ever performed?"

"My modern lit class at George Washington High read one aloud."

"That's *all*?"

"Look, the teacher said I was very promising."

"Don't you just hate that?" Della said. "It's like complimenting garbage for being a promising source of methane." Her fingers clutched one of the two notes I had hanging on the line "What's this say?"

"'Kim and I meet. Don't forget the ducks!'"

"What's that supposed to mean?"

"Kim's father was Portuguese and raised ducks in their backyard."

"Jeez, that has a ring of reality about it. Where'd you meet Kim?"

"At school during an explosion."

"Huh?"

"We were helping our science teacher when someone tried heating sulfur with benzene. That's when Kim and I said our first words to each other."

I started jotting down a note. By the time I finished, I looked up to see Della oiling the mannequin's neck.

"I'm glad you decided on the bed after all," she said.

The thought of Kim had pulled the breath out of me. Now, the sight of a blind girl greasing a big rubber dummy with Kim's nose and chin really threw me. I needed time to get my head together. I leaned to the right so my voice would seem like it was coming from the dummy.

"Kim had long, brown hair and dark, huge eyes like a calf."

"My father had eyes like a calf too."

"Kim was ashamed of being Portuguese, so she told everyone she was Australian."

"Did you make out with her in this room?"

"Not much. Kim only really got turned on at the Great Lawn in Central Park. She loved making out under blankets during Paul Simon and free rock 'n' roll concerts. She hated classical music."

Suddenly the bottle of oil slipped from her

hands and fell between the dummy and the comforter. As Della's hand shot out to find it, she accidentally grabbed the mannequin's hip.

"Oh my God!" she screamed, leaping away. "You've got no shorts on! Put shorts on immediately! What do you think I am?"

"I'm sorry. Look, I'm really sorry!"

"Shorts! Shorts! Put them on now! Immediately!"

I grabbed a pair of my BVD's out of a dresser, and wrestled them onto the mannequin. "I was caught up remembering Kim on the Great Lawn."

"I'll bet you were! You're going to turn out to be another teenage crazy, aren't you? I need another drink! A major vodka! Now!"

"Yes, of course." I ran out to the kitchen, poured her another shot, and rushed back to her. I touched the glass to her fingers, she clutched it and started lapping at it. "You forgot the lemon twist, didn't you?"

"Are you sure you should be drinking?"

"I'm sure. Are you decent yet?"

"Yes."

She polished off the vodka, set the glass down on the floor, and managed to grab the rubber neck again on the first shot.

"A lot of boys try to take advantage of me because I'm blind." She squirted more oil, but it hit the dummy's left ear. "Did Kim really love you? Like were you going steady?"

"She went out with other boys, if that's what you mean."

"She dated other boys while she dated you?"

"Yes."

"She *liked* other boys?"

"Sure."

Her eyebrows lifted above the dark glasses. "She told you about them?"

"No. *They* told me about *her*. But when she tried to jump out of Mrs. Midgeley's class window, I knew I'd failed her. She had needed me to be a stronger friend."

"Needed you to be a stronger friend? The more you tell me about this Kim, the more it sounds like what she really needed was shock treatments and a high-tech chastity belt. God! You want to know why you're blocked? You were hanging out with the wrong vampire. You're trying to write about a prime girl dork who didn't really love you. You've got to forget that loser and move on to writing about some kind of decent, terrific, faithful girl! Someone pretty and loving and exciting who can be a soulmate just for you. You need someone who can inspire you and really care about you! This Kim is a big, mixed-up, psychotic goose!"

"Kim was a special girl."

"Oh, she was special all right."

"It wasn't her fault she had dominating parents. Her mother was so powerful, she once crashed her Buick into a Volkswagen and single-handedly lifted the Volkswagen up off a college kid who was trapped underneath!"

"Enough already! I need to get the oil off your neck and get out of here!" She let go of the mannequin and grabbed a Ziploc plastic bag out of her gym satchel. It was filled with washcloths. "Here! Run these under hot water, wring them out, and bring them back."

"Della, I can't let you."

"Quick!" She shook the bag like a big white pom-pom. I took it. She slid onto the floor and started doing leg exercises.

"Let the water run as hot as you can stand it, and don't forget to wring out each one separately to keep the steam in! Hurry! Hurry! Hurry!"

I dashed out to the kitchen sink and put the washcloths under the hot-water tap. There were more than a dozen, and I had wrung out only two or three when I heard a *clank* from the hallway. I left the rest of the cloths under the splashing water and peeked around the corner.

Della was standing in front of my parents' liquor cabinet. One by one she grabbed bottles of booze and stuffed them into her gym bag. She worked fast, expertly, and was finished in seconds. I watched her run back to my room without any cane or dark glasses. At first, for some reason, I felt almost as sad as when I'd heard Daniel Barker had punched a school-bus driver and was being shipped off to a military prep school. My hopes for having someone to count on were disappearing again.

I went back to the sink and shut off the water. I wrung the washcloths out in one big, tangled mass like they were Della's neck.

It was clear I was the only one in my apartment who was blind!

◆◆◆◆◆

A little Madness in the Spring
Is wholesome even for the King.
—EMILY DICKINSON

Aaeeeyaaayaaayaaayaaa.
—TARZAN

◆◆◆◆◆

4

◆◆◆◆◆

I put the washcloths back in the Ziploc bag. I dried my hands on a paper towel. As I walked back to my room, all I could think of was a *Star Gazette* headline I had seen on a rack at a supermarket: MALIBU TEENAGER MAKES MEDICAL HISTORY BY LIVING A NORMAL LIFE WITH HALF A BRAIN!

Della was back on the floor pretending she'd been doing leg exercises the whole while. Next to her was the bulging gym bag.

"David?" she called, her dark glasses firmly back in place. "Are you there, David? David, where are you?"

I walked over to the gym bag. "I saw what you did."

"Oh, you're back."

Suddenly, I found myself yelling at her. "YOU'RE NOT BLIND! OH MY GOD! YOU'RE HORRIBLE!" I threw the Ziploc bag of washcloths down at her and started unloading my parents' liquor bottles. "Oh my God, my God! You've made a fool out of me. A complete, raving, stupid fool!"

Della sat up slowly. She took off her glasses, revealing huge blue eyes packed with makeup. "If I made you into the fool, then how come *I'm* the one who got to oil the dummy?"

"You're a thief, taking my folks' booze!"

"Yeah, well, I could have used some decent food, too. I'm sure the rest of your refrigerator's just like that disgusting shriveled old lemon peel you gave me."

"Get out of my apartment! Get out!"

"Oh, I'm out of here all right!"

She got up, grabbing her gym bag and cane. She headed toward the front door with me right behind her. She pointed at the photo of my grinning parents riding camels at the Morocco Club Med. "And if you think I'm impressed by Humpty Dumpty with Florence of Arabia, you're sadly mistaken."

"How dare you insult my mother and father,

you crook! You're a crook!"

"I'm not a crook! I'm not!"

"You are!"

She flung the door open and hurried to the elevator.

"I've got a baby to feed! I have a two-year-old baby girl to feed!" she spit over her shoulder, punching the button for the elevator.

"Baby girl, my foot!"

"I have so!"

"You've got some nerve inventing a baby. That's just another lie!"

"It is not! I have a daughter, the most beautiful baby on this earth!" She opened a locket that hung around her throat and thrust it into my face. There was a snapshot of a pathetic little baby holding a stuffed koala bear. *"See? See?"*

"Then get a respectable job."

"I can't hold a respectable job!"

She kicked the elevator doors. "I'm not going to stand here and be subjected to your vicious mouth!" She ran for the stairs. I followed her down the three flights.

"I've worked for a lot of producers," she said.

"I'll bet."

"I've done TV and a lot of things for my age.

Nobody's been hiring lately. It's not my fault. You were my first paid theater coaching job."

"So you lied about Joyce Carol Oates?"

"Of course I lied," she screamed as we reached the lobby. "If there's one thing Joyce Carol Oates does not have, it's writer's block!"

She didn't care who heard her, and she started swinging her cane in front of her again. "I'm desperate! I had no choice! My baby's from heaven. We have to live with my poor mother!"

"Let her take care of you then!"

"She can't. She's a poet on food stamps and she's in the middle of having a nervous breakdown. She's just like you, discarded by society."

In the lobby, Joe the doorman and an old lady with a Chihuahua stared at Della like she was crazy.

"Anything wrong, David?" Joe asked.

"No, Joe."

Della hit the revolving door and spun out onto the sidewalk. I went right after her.

"I am not discarded," I protested. "I'm too young to be discarded."

"Being called 'promising' in a high school English class ain't exactly being lionized."

"If your husband wanted a child bride, why

doesn't he support you?"

"I never had a husband." She began to cry and run down Broadway, dark glasses, cane, and all. Dozens of passersby stared. A Pakistani fruit seller on the corner almost dropped a whole sprig of bananas—nobody had ever seen a blind person travel at her speed!

"Hey, I'm sorry you had no husband," I said, running beside her.

"Don't be. I mated with a great guy. You've heard of Mel Gibson?"

I felt my eyes open as big as wagon wheels. "Mel Gibson fathered your baby?"

"No. Mel has a brother."

"Mel Gibson's brother fathered your baby?"

"No. But a boy who *knew* Mel Gibson's brother did. At least that's what he told me."

"Oh, you've got problems!"

"Yeah. But at least I'm not the one who's blocked!"

"Look, I'm a terrific writer for my age."

"Sure! I read all the time how Shakespeare's folios would have been nothing without his *clothesline of plot*!"

We stopped on the corner of Sixtieth Street. I thought she'd wait for a green light to cross over

Columbus Circle, but she didn't. She plowed out into traffic. Cars screeched and slammed on their brakes. Even the cement statues on the corner of Central Park looked startled.

"Help her! Help her!" a group of nuns in a Chevy Caprice station wagon called out to me.

I rushed and grabbed Della's arm, but she shook loose. We made it to the center island. She raced past the Columbus fountain, but I wasn't finished with her by a long shot.

"My clothesline works for me. You've got a major teenage alcohol abuse problem, that's what you've got!"

"Yeah," she huffed, folding her collapsible cane. She tossed it along with her sunglasses into her gym bag. "But if you weren't so strictured trying to write a dumb sob story for your nymphomaniacal, lamebrained girlfriend, you'd have noticed I have a Valium-gluttony-sugar-and-chocolate-abuse problem as well."

She showed signs of wearing out as we passed the Tang & Tang Noodle Shoppe at 58th street. By the end of the block she had to lean against a pole in front of the Papaya King Carrot & Passion Fruit Juice stand. She wouldn't look at me.

"You're not able to help me," I said. "You

can't even help yourself."

"I've helped plenty of my writer friends." She took out a tissue and blew her nose. "Lots who are much more talented than you are."

"You don't have any writer friends to help."

"Yes I do."

"Name one."

"Ed Weingarten."

"Who?"

"ED WEINGARTEN! ED WEINGARTEN! ED WEINGARTEN!" she yelled over the traffic like I was deaf.

"I've never heard of Ed Weingarten."

"He's the only kid with his own cable TV show, *Teen Time* on Channel 17. A lot of kids watch it."

"I don't."

"You're really out of it! His show ranks right behind all that stuff on Nickelodeon and those crumby network afternoon specials. He's got a variety show. Does anything he wants. He used to use a ventriloquist's dummy to interview teenage celebrities."

"It sounds crazy."

"Well, it wasn't. Ed could talk through the dummy a mile a minute, but on his own he was so frightened he was mute."

"How'd you help him?"

"I got him to cut the dummy." She headed on down Broadway. I kept beside her as the five P.M. rush-hour crowd began pressing in on us. "I got Ed Weingarten to trust his own instincts and fly," she said. "The dummy's been gone for over a year now, and Ed does all his own writing for the show, all the interviewing, and sometimes even a little song and dance. His girlfriend, Gabrielle Zacks, does a great news segment called 'The Sassy Edge.' Her uncle's the one with all the money. He helped Ed produce an off-Broadway play I starred in."

"What play?"

"*Mermaids Off Weehawken.*"

"It sounds awful."

"Oh sure, it flopped, but it was mainly because Ed Weingarten is a really terrible producer, even for a teenager. We closed in one night. I really adore Ed, but a producer he's not."

"You really unblocked him?"

"I know more about writing than I even do about acting. I'm able to get right inside the characters of a writer's mind and think like they do. I improvise. I do sense memory. I use physical gestures. Hey, even the doctors at Bellevue Hospital said I have a genius for storytelling."

"What doctors at Bellevue?"

"In the substance-abuse ward, not the psychiatric wing, *you wish!*"

Maybe she *could* help me. By this time I really wanted to know how she'd helped Ed Weingarten break through his block.

A drunk in a frilled orange vest kept flashing a sign in our faces that said SUPPORT SCIENCE! PLEASE DONATE ONE DOLLAR SO I CAN CONTINUE A MILLION DOLLARS' WORTH OF WINE RESEARCH! Show-offs on Rollerblades charged past us, a Dumpling King delivery boy on a bike practically ran us over, and a two-hundred-pound lady roared by in a motorized wheelchair.

"Can I treat you to a slice of pizza?" I asked Della.

"Look, a few minutes ago you were calling me a crook."

"Well, I was angry."

She hesitated. "All right."

I took her hand and helped her through the mob for another block, past Tony Roma's A Place for Ribs to the Cosmic Pizza Palace. We went in; I got a couple of slices with extra cheese from the counter, along with two Diet Cokes. We sat at an empty table in the window.

"So how'd you help Ed Weingarten?"

"I told him not to write or do anything artistic that didn't make him cry."

"Well, I cried for Kim."

"Oh, come off it. I'd have to be more than blind if I didn't catch on to the scene between you and that flying shish kebab. You never loved her, and she certainly never really loved you."

"She was my friend!"

"No way."

"Who are you to tell me that?"

"Look, dope, that's what you hired me for. One look at that room of yours and I knew the little zit-picker who lived there was way too uptight to have ever really cared for anybody. What with your neat little Magic Marker papers! Your Post-Its and pencils all in a row! You do everything by the numbers."

"Some people might call it professional."

She reached out for my chin with a napkin. "There's a piece of gross pizza gook hanging from your lip."

"Thank you."

She sipped her Diet Coke. "All you do is lie around in that apartment sobbing, 'Oh dear me, there's a mist falling on my terrace.'"

"I do not."

"Look, we're both sensitive. I know you don't need anyone else to tell you that emotionally you're a big zero. I'm sure you've gotten enough of that from Kim, and that mom-and-pop traveling circus you've got."

"Would you kindly shut up?"

"Oh, cut it. When you thought I was blind at least you talked to me with a little reality. Now you want me to shut up!"

"Please, be quiet."

"What? You think I'm some kind of Sony Walkman you turn off because you're finished jogging?" She took a bite from a piece of crust, wiped her hands with a napkin, and scooped up her hair. She fastened it into a big pile on her head with a plastic gizmo. "I'm not going to sit still and let you spin into some kind of control freak! You know what that is to me? It's very frightening. You're very frightening and cruel. That's what a boy is who can't show his feelings. You want me to take everything as my fault!"

"I just met you!"

"That doesn't matter. The whole effect is barbaric! I'm probably the nicest friend you've met in months, and that was by answering my ad and hiring me. Aren't you a catastrophe?"

I couldn't speak. I concentrated on a circle of dough the pizza cook was hurling into the air, spinning it bigger and bigger. He slapped it down on a floured board and pinched it around the edges as the jukebox blasted some cowboy singer crooning "All My Exes Live in Texas!"

"I feel so guilty about Kim," I said, finally.

"Why? What did you really do to her?"

"I wasn't me," I said. "I just wasn't me."

"What does that mean?"

"I always knew there was something wild and unstable about her."

"Then why did you go with her?"

"She was the only beautiful girl who paid any attention to me. She came after me."

"Didn't you know other girls?"

"Just plain ones."

"That wasn't their fault."

"No. They were nice girls. Their mothers and fathers were nice too. The girls only had personality."

"Personality's important."

"One girl I used to go out with, Peggy Sarzano, would play Rachmaninoff's Prelude in C Sharp Minor on the piano. She played it a lot because it was the only thing she knew. And this other girl I used to go out with, Cynthia Cumingdonger, got tickets to square dances. And Nora Dumbrowski always called me and tried to look pretty in ruffled blouses and earrings shaped like endangered species."

"They sound like sweet girls."

"They were, but no matter what kind of date we went on, we always ended up around the kitchen table with the girl and the mother laughing and complimenting me while they stuffed my face. It was like they were screaming, 'Oh god, David! David! Please love my poor homely daughter and be her boyfriend and don't notice she looks so drab.' I was desperate to have a friend who I could depend on, and be completely honest with, and who wouldn't disappear on me. Then I met Kim."

"You picked the gorgeous, lunatic slut."

"I went for flash. I feel terrible."

"Don't. Girls with personality always will find someone who really loves them. They end up marrying really good-looking plumbers and garage mechanics, have beautiful children, and spend nice summers in the Poconos." She got up and shoved our paper plates and soda cups into the trash bin. "Thanks for dinner, but I've got to get home to my baby."

She dashed out of the Cosmic Pizza Palace and headed back toward Columbus Circle, with me tagging along. The sidewalks were even more crowded with freaks and office workers rushing home. I could barely keep up with her. Guys were selling hot chestnuts and salted pretzels. Burger King had a banner flapping in the wind: GOOF TROOP BOWLING TOYS WITH THE PURCHASE OF A WHOPPER! We had to step over some boy in rags sitting on the sidewalk playing a samba on an electronic keyboard for donations.

"You know, I hate to tell you, David, but you're a very surface person," Della said above the din. "Even so, you didn't deserve getting stuck with Kim. If you've got to do some kind of playwriting kvetch about her, then memorialize the best part of her. She liked Central Park, so write a play with a lot of plants and bushes in it."

"She did love plants."

"You won't even be able to write about that in

that room of yours!" The beads on her dress lit up as we passed a blazing Pathmark Drugs window display of Speed Stick deodorant. "You've got nothing alive in your room! Nothing that throbs or jerks or cries out that it's breathing! Your whole apartment is like a tomb!"

She stopped at the edge of Central Park near the Fifty-ninth Street subway entrance. "You never really knew Kim," she said. "You let her get away without ever letting her know you. You let her date the other boys without telling her how you felt. You had to feel terrible she was seeing other guys. You had to feel rotten. You took second and third and last place because you didn't want to make any waves. If you ask me, I know Kim better than you ever did."

"You never met her!"

"Oh, forget her, her Portuguese father, and the ducks! The girl you should write about has a picture of her father next to her bed. Her father in an army uniform."

"What picture?"

"She's got an eight by ten of her dad in a frame flanked by two large polished mortar shells."

"Kim never kept a picture of her father next to her bed."

"But *I* do!"

She was starting to really freak me out. "You're telling me about *your* father?"

"Yeah. I'm telling you my father had his head blown off in a war when I was two years old, that's what I'm telling you."

"Look, I don't think I should listen to unsolicited ideas."

"Who are you kidding?" The wind blew the entire mass of her hair loose. She took her plastic hair gizmo and shoved it into her gym bag. "My father got exploded in a war and mucked up my flight plan."

"What flight plan?"

"The one my father would have given me if he had lived."

"How do I know you're not making all this up?"

"WHAT THE HELL DIFFERENCE WOULD IT MAKE?"

"I don't know."

She took my right hand. Slowly, she pressed it against her chest. She held it there, not caring if anyone passing saw us. "If you want, I'll let you cut into me with your writing, I'll breathe my life into your pages. You'll put me into your play. It'll be a story about me as a terrified young girl."

"How were you terrified?"

She dropped my hand and started walking in circles beside the park wall. A trio of nurses stared as they passed, probably heading for St. Luke's Hospital down the block.

"What's the matter?"

"I'm having a panic attack. I get shaky when I think about anything I shouldn't."

"Then don't think about it."

"Do you want to write a play or not?"

"I want to know how you were terrified."

She took several deep breaths and leaned against the stone wall. She pulled me close to her. "I didn't catch on until I was thirteen. I started getting irrational fears when I was with a boy."

"What kind of fears?"

"Crazy fears."

"Like what?"

"Like I was with one boy who tried to come on to me, and I started worrying about Mother Teresa and what a strain it must be to try to be nice all the time. That kind of thing. Then I went through this whole period of being overly concerned about underdogs. I'd be out to a movie with a boy and I'd find myself worrying that transvestites didn't have a significant fashion magazine."

"That was socially conscious of you."

"What really annoyed me was when a boy invited me to go on vacation with his family for a week in Boca Raton. My mom let me go, but on the flight I was afraid the flight attendants would be sucked out through the toilets."

"Oh."

"I was even afraid to go to my high school nurse, because I was afraid she'd chloroform me and put breast implants in me contaminated with salmonella. It was all so irrational."

"All this because you didn't have a father?"

"Let's just say in the loving department, my Cuisinart was missing a few blades."

"Did you see a therapist?"

"No. What I did was start studying couples."

"What'd that do?"

"I wanted to learn how to feel love. This boy by the name of Al came along. I learned about love from Al."

"Al *who?*"

"Al and Della," she said softly. "We fell in

love. I found out how powerful love can be between a boy and a girl."

"What was Al like?"

"It doesn't matter what *my* Al was like. I'm here to unblock *you*. You'll write your play, and we'll both come alive in it. We'll live! Someone will produce it and we'll become the most famous teenagers in theater. Real theater, forget the movies! You'll be the teenage dramatist. I'll be the star! Don't you realize there's never been a famous teenage playwright?"

A chill rushed down my back. "I'd like that."

"I've told you enough to write about me. Now you've got to write a boy in your play."

"I'm willing to do anything you say."

"I'm telling you! Let go of the emergency brake! You've been driving with the brake on. Forget that poor, demented girlfriend who tried to harpoon herself! Feel! You've got to *feel*! You've got to be the boy in this story."

"What are you talking about?"

"You're not writing any requiem! You're going to write a love story! A staggering story about teenage love in desperate times. I told you about Della! You create an unforgettable boy! Just get some plants in your room! Get palms and philodendrons! Teenage imbeciles can keep them alive!"

The leaves of the park trees rustled suddenly. She put her hands on my shoulders. "You just start writing a play you'd die for! You fill your whole room with my plants and my music! Get branches and Brahms! Skip the bubble-gum tunes. Bring out the big guns and make your place into an *un*bridled path!"

She grabbed a stick and began to write on a patch of sandy dirt. "If you've got to write something on your walls, you write the words 'RISE TO YOUR FULL VOICE BEFORE YOU'RE DEAD!'"

The lights of Columbus Circle bounced from Della's eyes like fire.

"Maybe I *could* try to write a love story."

She moved closer, completely ignoring the staring faces that poured past us like a river into the subway. "David," she whispered in my ear, "last night I dreamed I was backstage in a theater again. It was just a little high school play, but I was thrilled. I dreamed what it was like to be loved by a boy again. We're partners, David Mahooley. And in your play we'll be madly, completely in love!" She lowered her lips onto mine.

A hundred crazy images sprinted through my mind: the preserved head of a Mexican bandit some guy in Santa Rosa, California, keeps in a jar on a shelf; a slice of pizza with double cheese; bungee jumping from the Fuji blimp!

The kiss ended.

"My God, David Mahooley, you *are* cute!" she said, and fled down into the subway.

The mob swallowed her and she was gone.

I stood against the park wall for a long while. Then, slowly, I made my way back to my building and into the elevator. My brain was spinning as I entered the apartment. I walked by my mother and father grinning on the camels. I went to my room and sat down at my desk.

I could still feel Della's kiss on my lips as I began to type like a madman.

◆◆◆◆◆

One truth discovered is better than all the fluency and flippancy in the world.
　　　　　　　　　　　　　　—WILLIAM HAZLITT

No matter how thin you slice it, it's still baloney.
　　　　　　　　　　　　　　—ALFRED E. SMITH

•••••

5

•••••

That night I wrote for three hours straight. I took a break at ten to have a pepperoni-and-sausage pie delivered from Frank and Pepe's Pizzarama.

Della had stirred up a boiling pot of memories about Kim, and Daniel Barker, and practically any pal I ever had or even wanted. She made me remember Tommy Hill from my sophomore year, when we made a potato clock together for the science fair, but his mother got a heart attack dancing on a Caribbean cruise ship so they moved to Georgia. I guess I always had the worst luck picking kids I wanted to pal around with.

The eleven-o'clock TV news didn't help either in the downer department. The main stories were about a Perth Amboy groom torturing his bride with poisonous centipedes, a Bronx police-woman shooting her stepdaughter during a gun-safety lesson, and a report on how a San Diego teenage gang initiates its new members by kick-ing them and running and jumping on them un-til their ribs are broken. I guess a lot of the world was really nuts and lonely.

There was a particularly heavy mist hitting my terrace. I threw open the door, went out, and glared up at the terrace right above. "YOU'RE SPLASHING MY TERRACE AGAIN!" I yelled. I couldn't see anyone, but the giant mean schnauzers started barking like dog maniacs. "CAN'T YOU SHUT THOSE MUTTS UP! STOP SPLASHING MY TERRACE AND SHUT THOSE MUTTS UP! SHUT 'EM UP!"

Joe the doorman was working a double shift, so at one A.M. I brought him down a slice of pizza. I like talking to Joe, because he tells good fishing stories, and he listens to me whenever I have something to complain about.

"Catch anything lately?" I asked Joe.

"Yeah," he said, munching on the pizza. He always wears a pressed gray uniform with a fresh white shirt and bow tie. The other doorman, Horace, is always drunk and usually doesn't show up.

"I went fishing in a pond near Ellenville," Joe said, "and something big got on my line. I thought I had a twenty-pound catfish, but when I got it to the top it turned out to be a snapping turtle."

"How big?"

"Three feet with a head the size of a dinner plate."

"What'd you do?"

"I'll tell ya, David, I fell off this dam I was fishing on."

"What happened to the turtle?"

"I only had him hooked under the shell. It was an accident, so it got off. That was okay by me. You don't want to dredge up stuff like that."

"Right."

I made Joe tell me his favorite story about his father taking him bass fishing next to alligators in Lake Okeechobee. I always get a kick out of it. He also tells great bad jokes.

"Hey, David, what'd the teacher say when his glass eye slid down the drain?"

"What, Joe?"

"Whoops! I lost another pupil!"

After a while I went back upstairs. I was wondering if my parents had landed in Budapest safely. I checked for a message on the fax machine. There wasn't one, so I went back to writing my play.

The character of Della came along great, but every time I had to write something about me, I had a problem. Della's words came back to haunt me. Maybe I had never let Kim know who I really was, because I didn't even know myself.

Just before going to sleep, I thought about what I might have said to Kim. *Hey Kim, why did you go out with other guys behind my back, especially the football team? And Kim, I never should have told you I was afraid a meteor was going to hit the earth in our lifetime and destroy us like the dinosaurs. I loved the way you could say so much about foreign movies, Italian fashions,* The Scarlet Letter *and other books on our compulsory reading list. Kim, I'm sorry I never talked about you much. Not the real you. I should have told you I dreamed of marrying you one day and having kids. Kim, why didn't you tell me Danny Scarella knocked you up? And after Danny, why didn't you tell me Mike Funuzzi made you pregnant too! Why didn't you tell me about all the abortions you had because guys said they wouldn't marry you, which is why you tried to jump out Mrs. Midgeley's window! Kim, why couldn't we have been honest with each other? Why did we leave out so much? I didn't even know you had this need for demonstrative fertility.*

I should have told her what I thought when she'd call me at night and wanted to go out. If I didn't have the money, she'd steal it from her father's wallet or make me go with her while she rang doorbells to ask old lady parishioners to donate to the Our Sacred Lady Star of the Sea church building fund. I did tell her I thought that wasn't right. One night she borrowed someone's Hertz rental car and then just left it on a sidewalk outside the White Horse Tavern on Hudson Street. She'd drag me to SoHo afterhours joints where they'd serve beers to anyone. Kim would flirt with guys when we walked in, and they'd yell things like "Hey, honey, you slummin' tonight?"

Kim, why did you have to push everything as far as it could go? Why'd you never want to go home? Why wasn't I enough? Why didn't I tell you I saw you were going to hell in a hand basket?

Finally, I dreamed of Della's kiss.

◆◆

The next day in school I wasn't tired. Two percent of my brain handled the classwork. The rest of my mind made notes about Della Jones and my play.

After school, I typed for nine and a half hours straight. Then I wrote the whole weekend. The story was about a boy called Al falling in love with a girl called Della. If Della didn't like me using her real name, I'd change it. I put the best of everything I knew about myself into the character of Al, and finished stacks of pages each day.

Della's character practically wrote itself. I'd close my eyes and see her waterfall of hair, her elegant nose, and her massive eyes. I began collecting plants for my room. I bought four ferns, an "old man" cactus, and three split-leaf philodendrons on sale at Woolworth's. I found a box of half-dead geraniums sitting out for the garbage in front of Loews Broadway cineplex. When Joe saw me lugging the geraniums into the building, he put me onto three other half-croaked plants in the basement that some tenants had thrown out.

On Monday when I woke up there was a message waiting on the fax machine:

Dear David,

We love Budapest. The goulash is to die! There are lines at McDonald's and Adidas stores from dawn to 3 a.m. Men, women, and children here love Levi's Button-Fly Jeans! How are you? Dad says don't leave too many lights on. We've picked up another assignment. The International Herald Tribune is interested in us doing a story on spas of Austria. Tomorrow we take the hydrofoil up the Danube to Vienna. Juicy wiener schnitzels, here we come! Our fax there is the Strauss Hotel 011 43 103–45828. Hope you are fine and finally over Kim Stark. Dad said to remind you that you didn't drive her psycho. We've changed flights to Oct. 18. Miss you. If you need more money, use your automatic teller card. We'll reimburse you when we get back. Love and kisses. Drink orange juice. More kisses.

Love,
Mom and Dad

I stuck the message in a special "Parents' Fax" folder I keep under my mattress. I saved their faxes from Tahiti, San Francisco, Dublin, Mount Vesuvius, Athens, Hawaii, Kenya, Puerto Rico,

Devonshire, Monaco, Singapore, Barcelona, Moscow, Tasmania, Madagascar, Oklahoma, Myrtle Beach, and Perth Amboy. Someday if I do get married and have kids, they'll probably learn more about their grandparents from that fax folder than from anything else.

Exactly a week after Della unblocked me, I wanted to let her know the play was coming along. I dialed the Student Theater Coach number. A computer voice said, "The number you have reached, 555–4827, has been disconnected." What a bummer.

I called directory assistance, but they had no Della Jones listed. Then I figured the phone might be listed under her mother's name, so I checked all the Joneses who had first names that sounded like lady poets. Theda. Esmeralda. Zuba. I called a dozen Joneses, but with no luck. I didn't like not knowing how to get in touch with Della. It wasn't that I needed her immediately, because I was still fired up and writing like there was no tomorrow. I just knew the day would come when I'd want her to read my pages.

A lot of my teachers noticed my spirits had really picked up, and I was keeping up with all my homework and quizzes.

"I'm glad you're speaking up in class again," Miss Conlan, my English teacher, told me. "Your essay on hypocrisy, false values, and the world as a comic hell was very, very good."

"Thanks."

All the kids really respect Miss Conlan because she's sharp as a tack and used to work at *The New York Times*. She's also the faculty advisor for the school paper, *The Crow's Nest*.

"Are you writing any new plays?" she asked.

"I'm working on one now."

"What's it about?"

"It's a love story."

"I'm glad. I always thought one day, after you finished with space monsters and flesh-eating children, you'd write a really good love story."

"I'm sure this play's going to be professionally produced," I said.

"I'll keep my fingers crossed."

"It's got a great part for Meryl Streep." The words were no sooner out of my mouth than I wanted to kick myself.

"Meryl Streep? Oh my." She smiled. "That's wonderful. Do you mind if I pass that little tidbit along to the gossip editors?"

"*Variety* ought to be printing an item about it soon," I invented. It was like I couldn't stop making things up. I did think the play was starting to look very professional. Besides, who knew? A famous actress like Meryl Streep probably would give her eyeteeth to play a great character like Della. What if I never could find Della again? I mean, that was a possibility. What if she had taken off to live in Cleveland or Utah? With her anything was possible. Besides, almost every friend I ever had usually disappeared to someplace sooner or later.

The next Friday I passed the same Columbus Avenue flea market where I had bought the dummy. There was a set of three beat-up little drums and a cymbal gizmo.

"They're Caribbean drums," the guy at the stand said. He shoved a pair of drumsticks at me. "Try 'em. You can hit 'em with all kinds of sticks and things."

I gave them a couple of smacks. They sounded good. I thought maybe they'd loosen me up even more for my writing. It was only sixteen bucks for everything, so I bought them and took them home with me on the bus. That night I put a Chopin etude on my CD player. It was very soothing to tap out a gentle beat right along with the piano music.

During the daytime when I was scribbling Post-Its and hanging new ideas on my Clothesline of Plot, I kept one eye on the TV. I had started watching Ed Weingarten's show. I wanted to get a look at the boy Della said she had helped. There he was, actually hosting his own afternoon Channel 17 *Teen Time* show. Ed had long brown hair, which he kept scooping out of his face like a rock star. He looked a little on the intense side, but he seemed very sincere. I wondered what he was like when he used to talk only through a ventriloquist's dummy. His girlfriend, Gabrielle Zacks, did a nice job on the teen news segment, "The Sassy Edge," and she and Ed looked like a perfect couple.

Ed Weingarten's show was on for two hours every weekday afternoon, so I'd watch a little, write, then go back and watch some more. I was hoping Della Jones would show up as a *Teen Time* guest, since she said she knew Ed Weingarten so well, but I didn't see her.

By October 7, at eleven o'clock in the morning, I had finished more than three quarters of the play. I made myself a cappuccino and started reading everything from beginning to end so I could really catch the flow. When I finished, I wanted to spew.

The character of Della was great.

Al was still a geek.

Unfortunately, Al was me. It was the worst feeling I had ever had in my life. I found out that I was somebody I didn't want to be because he was too dumb. By eight P.M. I went to bed. I was turning back into cement. "Where are you?" I silently prayed to Della. "Where are you, now that I need you so badly?"

At three A.M. the phone rang. I reached out for the receiver like swimming back from the dead. "Hello?"

"David?"

I bolted upright.

"Della?"

"Yeah," she said.

"Thank God you called!"

"Thank God? You really thank God?"

"I've been trying to find you."

"Have you? Have you really been trying to find me?"

"Yes!"

"What for?"

"I need to see you." There was a long pause. "Della, are you still there?"

"Oh, I'm here all right."

"I need you to come up here. I finished the play. I've got plants and drums! I've got so many things to show you."

There was another long silence.

"I'll meet you at the zoo," she said.

"What zoo?"

"In Central Park. That'll be more convenient than, say, meeting at a zoo in *Chicago*," she said. "At the front turnstiles."

"What time?"

"Noon, tomorrow. *Be there.*"

She hung up.

◆◆◆◆◆

I never know how much of what I say is true.
—BETTE MIDLER

♦♦♦♦♦
6
♦♦♦♦♦

I hadn't been to the Central Park zoo since it had all been rebuilt and they changed its name to the Wildlife Conservation Society. Everything was new to me. The administration building at the main entrance had been spruced up. It was once a famous arsenal. Now the front archway was decorated with a cement eagle, fake cannonballs, swords, and spears. It was there I noticed an omen. Two of the arsenal's entrance lights were in the shape of *drums*. I felt fate wanted me to be there, because one of the few things I had decided to bring along in my back-pack was my mid-size Caribbean drum.

There was hardly anyone else at the zoo except

for two employees hiding behind a rhododendron bush sneaking a smoke. Right at twelve I saw Della near the arsenal building. She wore a black trench coat, had Cleopatra eye makeup and blood-red lipstick on, and had her massive hair piled atop her head like a haystack. She lugged a heavy-looking, beat-up cloth shopping bag that bulged like it might contain a bomb.

"Hi," I said.

"Did you buy the tickets?"

"I'll get them."

It cost me five dollars for two admissions. Della led the way through the turnstile.

"Let me help carry your bag."

"Forget it."

"I wanted to show you everything I've done. I've got seventy-three pages of script. Lots of plants. I taped eight segments of the Ed Weingarten show on my VCR!"

She walked us quickly by a sign:

DO NOT THROW COINS IN THE SEA LIONS' POOL! COINS CAN KILL! THEY LODGE IN STOMACHS AND CAUSE ULCERS, INFECTIONS, AND DEATH!

We walked by a statue of a lioness chewing a peacock's neck, with two cubs at the base shoving each other to get a piece of the action. The whole zoo was very new, with brick columns topped by wooden arches and big slabs of transparent glass. There were ponds all over the place. One father stood on a bridge holding his little son over a stack of bulrushes.

"Let's see if we can see a frog," the father said.

"Here, froggie! Here, froggie!" the kid kept screeching.

Della marched us past the sea lions into a building called the Edge of the Icepack. The first stop she made was smack in front of a giant fifty-foot tank of really freaked-out penguins. We were the only two humans watching three hundred chinstrap penguins chatter, dive, and waddle all over the place. They acted like we had a few dozen flounders in our pockets ready to feed them.

Della set her shopping bag down with a loud thud next to the railing.

"Della, I called the number from your ad, but it was disconnected."

"Yeah, my mother and I went broke and couldn't pay the bill. My poor baby almost starved to death. What do you or the telephone company care?"

She took off her coat. She was wearing a full length black dress covered in sequins. I had never seen a girl look so beautiful except once when Miss America got out of a stretch limo at Lincoln Center and nearly got trampled to death by fans.

"Della, you look really great."

She focused her blue eyes on me like lasers. "I just came from a funeral. You think I look 'really great' for a funeral?"

"Who died?"

"It doesn't matter who died. You figured you were never going to see me again. You thought I was dead and buried."

"I tried to get in touch with you. Your phone was disconnected. You disappeared."

"Yeah, that's what you hoped for."

"No."

"You sucked my brain dry, and then I'm out of the picture! Well, that's not the way it works, David Mahooley. That's not the way show business works!"

"Della, I even called Bellevue. I asked if you were in the substance-abuse ward, and they said you weren't."

"Did you ask for me in the Teenage Detoxification Unit? Did you ask for me in Detox?"

"No."

"Because that's where I was! I went straight from our happy session at Columbus Circle into the teen detoxification ward."

"I'm sorry. Am I supposed to feel it was my fault?"

"Yes."

"Hey, you charged me good money, and now you're going to say I'm the one who drove you to drink? Is that what you're saying?"

"Bingo."

"I don't think that's fair." She turned to tap the glass at a big, fat penguin showing off for her. I noticed there was a split in her dress almost all the way up her thigh. "You wore *that* dress to a funeral?"

"You don't like it? It's an old costume. All the clothes I have are old costumes. I wore this in a Henry Street Settlement production of *The Good Woman of Setzuan*." Her voice broke.

"Della, who died?"

"My shrink."

"You didn't tell me you had a shrink."

"I *didn't* have a shrink." She began to pace the length of the huge penguin tank. They shrieked louder and swam so fast half of them flew out of the water. "One visit with you to play grease the dummy, and I needed a therapist!"

"Hey, I didn't drive you to drink or to a shrink."

"I went straight from spilling my guts on your floor into a freak-out that ended me up in Bellevue Detox!"

"It's not my fault."

"I thank God, actually, that I went to Detox because I ended up getting three weeks of therapy out of it, thanks to you."

"They gave you a free shrink?"

"There was a notice on the Bellevue bulletin board saying they needed alcoholic teen volunteers for a sobriety experiment. I ended up signing on to live with a bunch of other recovering kids in a brownstone on East Twenty-third Street. It was kind of intensive. They stuck electrodes in us while we slept."

"That's awful."

"No, it wasn't awful. It helped me. It helped all of us!"

"I'm sorry your shrink died. At least you weren't going to him for very long."

"Were you listening to me? I went to him for three weeks, four sessions a day, that's twenty-eight sessions a week! I bellyached my soul out to a psychoanalyst who decides to get killed on a commuter flight to Mamaroneck!"

"You make it sound like he *wanted* to get killed. Where was the funeral?"

"St. John the Divine. Hundreds of his teenage patients showed up. Look, I only have twenty minutes. I have to get back to the brownstone and meet my new shrink."

"The funeral must have been traumatic for all the kids."

"Of course it was traumatic. Half his poor outpatients broke down during the eulogy. Bellevue had buses waiting outside. What do you care? Just what do you care!" Della burst into tears.

A mother came through the doors rolling her baby in a stroller.

"Oh my, look at all the penguins," the mother said. "Aren't they cute?"

The kid looked wide eyed at Della in her black sequined dress.

"Penguin, penguin," he muttered, pointing straight at Della.

"No, I am not a penguin!" Della said. She grabbed her shopping bag and stormed out.

I ran after her. She charged over to the Polar Circle and stopped at an exhibit of arctic foxes.

"Della," I said softly, "maybe you'll feel better if you just have a really good cry."

"I'm not going to feel better. When I first heard that my shrink died, I was glad! Can you imagine how guilty that made me feel?"

"You weren't really glad he died."

"No, but I had mixed emotions about it because I had gone to him for over fifty sessions before I noticed he was a dwarf!"

"Your therapist was a dwarf?"

"And he never told me."

"Didn't you look at him?"

"David! People don't look at their therapists!"

"Well, I can understand why you're so upset, to find out your shrink is tiny—and dead, of course."

Della turned her huge, weeping eyes straight at me. I put my arm around her. I thought it might take her mind off things if I read her the zoo sign about the foxes.

"It says arctic foxes have the warmest fur of any animal, that they're fine even at forty degrees below zero."

"Who cares?" Della said.

"Don't you like animals?"

"Not much."

"Then why'd you want to meet at the zoo?"

"None of your business."

She shook my arm off like it was a snake and grabbed her shopping bag. She yanked a newspaper out of it and shoved it into my face. I couldn't believe it was a copy of *The Crow's Nest*, my high school newspaper! She poked her finger at its gossip column. There was the Meryl Streep item Miss Conlan told me she was going to put in.

I was stunned. "Where did you get *The Crow's Nest*?"

"Why? You think George Washington High has no drunks? You think your school has no booze freaks? You think there are no kid alcoholics from Stuyvesant, Brooklyn Tech, or the Bronx High School of Science? The Brownstone Experiment has kids from all over the city!" She set her shopping bag down. Again it made a loud *thud*!

"What do you have in your bag?"

"What do you want to know for?" Her tears stopped. She blew her nose in a tissue.

"It sounds heavy."

"Yeah, well the heavy thing is going to be a little surprise for you."

"You say that like it's a gun, or a bomb."

"Should it be, David? Is that what you think? Did you say anything about *our* play in your crumby little school newspaper that would make you think I'd come here with a gun?"

"Della, I swear I tried to get in touch with you. I was afraid something had happened to you, that you were too good to be true. I thought of nothing but you. Honest. I got plants the way you told me. I even got drums to help me open up even more. I play them!"

I sat down on a bench and pulled out the drum and my Sony tape recorder from my backpack. I shoved in a preset cassette and pressed the "play" button. The first movement of "The Moonlight Sonata" started, and I drummed along with it. It really perked up the arctic foxes.

"You unblocked me!" I told her, without missing a beat. "I even play drums for the plants. I watched the Ed Weingarten show. I didn't know if you'd be on it. Who knew?"

"Stop talking about Ed Weingarten. He's my friend, not yours!"

"I don't understand why you're so angry with me," I said. My drumming made Beethoven sound great, I thought. "The philodendrons love it when I drum to Mozart."

"Stop it!" she shrieked. "Stop it! You're out of your mind! Out of it!"

◆◆◆◆◆

My music is best understood by children and animals.
—IGOR STRAVINSKY

*I have never loved another person the way
I loved myself.*
—MAE WEST

What a time! What a civilization!
—CICERO (106–43 B.C.)

◆◆◆◆◆

7

◆◆◆◆◆

Della cleared out of the arctic foxes exhibit in a flash. It took me a couple of seconds to jam my drum and tape recorder back into my backpack. I dashed out the swinging doors into a labyrinth of hallways.

Della had disappeared.

I ran up a flight of wooden stairs. Suddenly, a huge, live polar bear reared up on its hind legs, pulled its lips back from its monstrous teeth, and swung its clawed arms out at my face. I screamed and jumped back. When my head hadn't been knocked right off my body, I realized the beast was behind a thick slab of floor-to-ceiling Plexiglas.

I ran on past onto an open-air viewing platform. Two larger bears paced near the edge of a deep tank surrounded by tremendous stalagmites of ice. All three of the bears had balding heads with glaring black eyes and white bodies marred by battle scars.

Della stood in a corner drying her eyes in front of a sign that read:

THE BEAR FACTS OF LIFE! IT IS BEARLY
BELIEVABLE BUT TRUE THAT POLAR BEARS
USE BIG CHUNKS OF ICE TO BREAK IN THE
ROOFS OF SEAL DENS. ONLY THE KODIAK
BROWN BEAR RIVALS THE POLAR BEAR AS
THE LARGEST CARNIVORE ON LAND!

I went to her.

"I thought you'd be pleased by the way the play was coming along," I said.

"You thought I'd be pleased you got your moronic school rag to print a lousy little gossip-column item about *our play*? You thought I'd be happy to read that 'David Mahooley has a new play that he thinks will lure Meryl Streep back onto the New York stage'? Are you out of your mind?"

"I made that up. The faculty advisor wanted

to encourage me by putting something in the school newspaper."

"You figured you had milked me dry and I'd vanish—POOF—leaving you with my ideas and my character? I may be sixteen, but I'm an Actors Equity pro, baby. A pro!"

She started down the stairs. I followed her as she headed toward a large outdoor pond at the rear of the zoo grounds.

"You're great, Della. I did everything you said." I grabbed the pages of the script out of my backpack and shoved them into her hands. She took them reluctantly, started looking through them as we walked. "Your role's terrific."

"It better be." She led us around the edge of the pond. Aeration gizmos made the deep, black water churn like a cauldron.

Two big, powerful swans with thick necks swam toward us. They halted offshore with beaks that looked like they could tear our faces off.

Della sat down on a bench facing the pond. She started reading like a madwoman.

"You've got great speeches!" I said. "I just haven't been able to write the character of Al very well."

"Writing an Al was the one thing you were supposed to do! I gave you me! And remember, you are writing this part for me, not Miss Meryl Streep! I could smack you! Just smack you!"

I backed off so she could concentrate on reading. A waterfall was to the left and behind the swans. I looked up and gasped. At the back of the pond was a sheer cliff of black rocks. Dozens of curious hairy faces with dark eyes stared down at me.

I moved quickly to the railing. There was a series of four sketches with a description of the exhibit.

JAPANESE SNOW MONKEYS: THE SNOW MONKEY CAN LIVE AT TEMPERATURES BELOW FREEZING. THEY ARE THE MODEL FOR ALL THE LITTLE STATUES ABOUT THE BUDDIST PROVERB "HEAR NO EVIL, SEE NO EVIL, SPEAK NO EVIL." THEY SURVIVE IN WINTER BY EATING BAMBOO AND EVERGREENS, WHICH THEY DON'T EAT IN ANY OTHER SEASON. YOUNG FEMALE MONKEYS STAY WITH FEMALE MONKEYS. YOUNG MALES FORM ROUGH-AND-TUMBLE PLAY GROUPS. LOSERS OF JUVENILE GAMES USUALLY END UP AS SUBORDINATE ADULTS.

That last bit of news scared me.

Finally, Della looked up.

"You're right," she said sadly. "This Al is a putz."

"I'm sorry. I guess there's going to be no play without you telling me about the real Al."

"You couldn't write about the real Al."

"Why not?"

"You're too uptight."

"I'm not!"

The afternoon sunlight crashed down, lighting her hair and sequins like neon. I sat next to her on the bench. "Della, I feel something for you. Something more than I've ever felt for anyone. Any girl or friend or pal I ever dreamed of having. There's a pain just over my heart ever since I first met you."

"Try Maalox or Rolaids."

"No. You've got me wrong, Della."

"I wish I did. I wish I was wrong, because I had another dream. When I was alone and hurting in the brownstone, when I was at rock bottom, I dreamed of you. You were wearing a Day-Glo yellow spandex swimming suit, and you were surfing with killer whales. All right, in that dream they did try to eat you, but in another dream, I found you very magical and kind."

She grabbed her shopping bag and lugged it closer to her. It made a loud *thuuuud* again when she sat it down on the bench. "Do you really think I have a gun or a bomb in here?"

"Do you?"

She reached into her bag and pulled out a large container of hair mousse. Suddenly, she squirted a huge glob of it on my head. She started massaging it into my scalp. "Your hair was driving me crazy! It's too dry. This is the perfect conditioner mousse. You don't even have to shampoo it out."

Her fingers rubbed the slop from around my ears and brow. I looked up to the cliff, and for a moment the whole pack of Japanese snow monkeys had stopped picking nits off each other and were staring at us. It looked like they were each keeping one eye on us for pointers.

"What's in this mousse?"

"Water, oil, and goat placenta."

"Goat placenta?"

"Al loved it. We'd put it on each other—you know, mutual grooming like gorillas do."

"Is that why we're here at the monkey cliff?"

"In a way," she said. "I suppose I knew you wouldn't be able to write Al. Zoos always remind me of Al."

Her voice faded. She grimaced in pain. She took her hands from my hair and turned to face the cliff, then lowered her gaze to the ground.

"I've got to leave. I need to get back to the brownstone. They'll assign me a new shrink who looks like Toto the Kissless Bride."

She didn't make a move to stand, only lifted her eyes to the monkeys again.

Instinctively, I grabbed the can of hair mousse and sprayed a glob of it on Della's head exactly like she'd done to me. "Al rubbed your head like this?" I asked, my hands dripping. "You rubbed each other's heads?"

"Wait." Della struggled to stop the gook from dripping into her eyes. My fingers burst her hair loose from its moorings. It spilled downward. I kept one hand massaging her scalp while my other hand pulled globs of mousse along the longest strands.

"I know this isn't coming out right," I said, "but all I've thought about was what I'd do if I ever found you again. Maybe we could go steady."

"David, the one thing I don't need in my life just now is an *in*significant other."

"But I want to care about you, to be as close as Al was with you."

"You can't."

"Just tell me what he was like, what he did and felt. I'll be able to feel it too."

"Al was Love jumping at my throat like a jaguar. Could you be that, David? Could you?"

"I could try. I could. Where did you meet him?"

She wiped a glob of mousse from her left cheek. "Al and I were guests on *Teen Time* with Ed Weingarten."

"Al was an actor too?"

"No, Al was a writer."

"So we're both writers. We've got to be alike. What was different about him?"

"He only wrote stories and poems about wild animals. He was on *Teen Time* because he wrote a poem about Montana wolves."

The kid who had thought Della was a penguin was out of his stroller and came waddling up to the railing next to us.

"Swans," the kid yelped, "swans!"

His mother was more fascinated by Della and

me massaging mousse into each other's heads. A few other parents and kids headed our way.

"Follow me," Della said, grabbing her still-heavy shopping bag. We skirted the left side of the pond to an incline snaking up behind the monkey cliff. The path broke open into a circle with a great view of the New York skyline.

"This is my secret spot," she said, leading me to a gazebo. We went in and sat down. The snow monkeys had followed our every move and now squatted not more than a dozen feet away. Only a narrow chasm separated us. The monkeys settled down again, stared at us, and went on with their business of grooming. They were so close now, I could see they were actually nibbling on the nits like pistachio nuts.

I reached out and took Della's hand. "You and Al met on Ed Weingarten's show?"

"Yes."

"What happened then?"

"To be blunt, we both picked each other up. After the show we went to Serendipity's for a frozen hot chocolate. Then he took me to this ritzy apartment he was minding for someone. He told me it once belonged to Jack Nicholson."

"You hung out with him in the apartment?"

"We went steady. One day a rich movie director next door sent over a fifty-pound sculpture of Godiva chocolate made in the shape of a life-sized woman's leg. Once I even caught sight of Liza Minnelli in the elevator."

"How old was Al?"

"Seventeen. David, don't try to be Al. I'm just telling you this so you can finish your play. Al wasn't like you. He was into nature."

"Was he the father of your kid?"

"No. My baby was six months old when Al and I met."

"He loved animals?"

"Yes. Al even wanted us to make out like different types of animals. One day we made out like alligators. The next day we loved each other like anteaters. Al had gravity boots, so once we even hung upside down in a closet and made out like African fox bats. Look, I'm not telling you this to make you jealous."

"I'm not jealous."

But I was.

"Al and I were completely in love. For the first time in my life I felt my mind and body was like an elodea plant, one of those water plants that can line up next to another elodea plant and build a bridge of cells to connect them."

"I don't know what you're talking about."

"I mean that when I was with Al, when our bodies touched, my insides melted. All of me flowed into him, and all of him into me. Oh, David, it's a blinding, shocking feeling that makes your blood blaze. You feel you're going to live forever. I don't think you'll ever know what really passionate human love is."

I let go of her hand.

"Della, don't you think that's a heartless thing to tell me?"

"I need to be truthful about it." Della shook her head so her hair scattered evenly across her shoulders as the conditioner dried. "Besides complete, transcendent love, we had a social life, too. We hung out with teenage movers and shakers."

"Like who?"

"Ed Weingarten became a personal friend of ours. I did dramatic readings on his show, and sometimes Ed and Gabrielle would stop over and we'd have hamburgers or pigs-in-the-blanket."

"Can I meet Ed?"

"What for?"

"If he produced you in one play, maybe he'll

produce you in my play."

"Look, Ed Weingarten is a great friend, but I told you he's incompetent as a producer!" She raised her voice, spooking a couple of the baby monkeys. They hid their eyes and clung to their mothers. "Ed's production of *Mermaids Off Wee-hawken* got a standing *booing* ovation!"

"Why is he such a terrible producer?"

"Ed's main problem is he and Gabrielle got into some very far-out social-political experiment. It's too freaky and bizarre to go into right now. Besides, I thought you wanted to know about Al."

"I do."

"Give me your foot."

"My foot?"

"Yeah."

Della grabbed my right foot and swung it up onto the gazebo bench. The monkeys watched as she made me lean back. She took off my shoe and sock.

"What are you doing?"

She held my foot like it was a specimen. "Now, a foot is a stupid thing, unless you're in love. When you're in love a foot becomes something special. You've got to feel this or you won't be able to write about it."

"I *want* to feel it."

"When you're in love with someone, you adore the strangest parts of them," she said, rubbing my foot. "Al was a tall, blond god. An aura radiated from his skin. I loved Al's large, beautiful feet. Sometimes we'd go to the movies and we'd hold each other's feet."

"You went to the movies and held *feet?*"

"Yes."

"I'll hold your feet."

"No."

I twisted around and pulled Della's left foot up onto the bench. Her shoe came right off, and I began rubbing her toes.

"You're twisting my ankle."

"Sorry."

The monkeys all stopped picking nits and really stared at us now.

"David, you're too mechanical. To make Al come alive in your play, you've got to write about teenage love the way it really is. It's hot! Burning! Boiling! I adored more than Al's feet. I loved kissing his beautiful hair. I loved him racing after me around the apartment. I grew to love his mind, his every thought. He was brilliant. He was graduating with honors from Bronx Science. I loved the way he cooked beef and Chinese pea pods in a wok. I worshiped the way he ate ribs. I was proud he was a holistic gourmet and knew the yin and yang of foods. He taught me that if you have a white tongue in the morning, you have to eat more protein that day, and a dark tongue means you have to eat more vegetables."

"He sounds too good to be true."

Several of the monkeys moved closer to us at the edge of their cliff. They looked like they could leap right over at us.

"I loved Al even when he told me he was from another world, that he was a teenage member of the genius society Mensa—but from another planet."

"Al told you he was a member of Mensa from *another planet*?"

"Oh, David, Al was just a little prone to exaggeration, but it doesn't mean he wasn't sincere."

"No, it means he was nuttier than granola!"

"Al's world was truer than any I had ever known before. A lot realer than other supposedly normal kids' worlds."

"Then why aren't you still with him? How did you split up?"

"That you don't have to know about. You can't write about our breaking up because it was a little irregular."

"Irregular?"

Her face flushed with pain, and her voice faded. She turned away from me. Her hands grasped at the air.

"Della, what's wrong?"

"I have to go," she finally was able to say.

We put our socks and shoes back on. She stood up and folded her coat over her arm. Two of the Japanese snow monkeys began to chatter at us like they didn't want us to leave.

"Please don't go," I said.

"I've got to get back to the brownstone. You just write about Al and me in love like I told you. You don't have to know any more. That's the only part any audience will want to hear."

"Don't leave."

"I've got to."

Several of the monkeys rushed forward to join the others. They chattered at us and made slapping sounds on their heads and chests.

"That reminds me," she said, reaching into her shopping bag. "I was afraid with your parents gone you weren't eating right and you might be anemic." She lifted out a huge frozen turkey.

"They were giving out free turkeys at the St. John the Divine soup kitchen after my shrink's funeral. I picked one up for you. Cook it in the oven at 325 degrees about five hours, until the thermometer doodad pops up." She plopped the cold, stiff carcass onto my lap and rushed from the gazebo.

The whole cliff of monkeys started screeching now, like they were crying *"Don't go! Don't go!"* Maybe they wanted the turkey.

I stood up holding her gift. I was really touched that she thought of me. I grabbed my backpack and ran after her down the hill.

"You need this for your mom and baby," I called, waving the turkey at her.

"No. They hate poultry."

I jogged to keep up with her as she rushed by the swans, the Polar Circle, and the sea lion pool. The sun was lower in the sky, hitting Della so every inch of her glistened. She ran past the statue of the lioness eating the peacock, around the old arsenal building, and out to the bus stop on Fifth Avenue.

I put my arm around her as she waited for the bus. "Della, I *need* to have feelings or I'll die!"

"Correction," she said. "You need feelings or you're not going to have any play."

I grabbed her and kissed her. It was not like our first kiss at the subway. This time I felt blinded and hot and passionate. Her body shivered in my arms.

"The turkey's melting on my leg," she said as her bus coughed to a stop. Its compressed-air doors sprang open with a gasp.

Della dashed up the steps.

"I need to know the *irregular* part about you and Al. The irregular!" I called to her. The driver looked at me like I was out of my mind.

Della spun around to face me. She looked terrified.

"Remembering that would make me cry blood, David. Is that what you want—for me to cry blood?"

The doors wheezed shut and the bus lunged forward, leaving me on the curb. I ran after the bus. It had to stop for a light at Sixty-first Street. Della sat at a window seat. I rapped on the glass. She looked at me.

"I'm going crazy," I shouted. "I don't know if I'm falling in love with you so I can write, or if I'm writing just so you'll fall in love with me."

She opened the window and stuck her head out.

"Hey, don't sweat it," she said. "As

Scheherazade used to say, 'If it ain't broke, don't fix it!'"

The light changed. Della slammed shut the window as the bus spit a cloud of black smoke at my feet. It pulled off and hurtled downtown.

A small crowd of tourists were staring at me. I didn't know why, until I remembered Della's gift. I looked down at the big, dripping bird in my hands and felt madly in love.

◆◆◆◆◆

O wad some Pow'r the giftie gie us
To see oursels as others see us.
——ROBERT BURNS

If you get to be a really big headliner, you have
to be prepared for people throwing bottles
at you in the night.
——MICK JAGGER

◆◆◆◆◆

8

◆◆◆◆◆

I t wasn't until I put the turkey into the oven that night that I realized I'd forgotten to get Della's home address again. She did say she was going back to the brownstone on East Twenty-third Street—but there are hundreds of brownstones there. I kicked myself, but I was still too delirious from the zoo to worry about it. To me, Della was magical. When I needed to find her again, I would! I'd find her when I deserved her!

While the turkey cooked, I did things I hadn't done since Kim had left. I started singing a song I remembered Mom and Dad singing when they used to be normal and stayed at home once in a while. We'd do things together. We'd go to a movie and sit down for regular meals and be a real family. I could hum the whole thing, but I never got the words right. It was a big-band song about falling in love and "seeing the light"!

The smell of the turkey cooking even got me to clean my closet. I came across my old empty fish tank. I remembered I asked for it the first time my folks said they were taking off, for Australia, and leaving me with my Aunt Frieda. Aunt Frieda was nice enough, except I heard she had once required psychiatric care and she constantly threatened that if I didn't eat my rice pudding, she'd put me in her cellar, where monster spiders lived.

I remember trying to figure out why my mom and dad were always taking off, and I finally decided it was because of TV news programs, PBS specials, and docudramas. They used to be happy staying at home and watching movies like *101 Dalmatians*, *Gone With the Wind*, and *E.T.* They'd make big bowls of caramel popcorn and rent *Pinocchio* and *Night of the Living Dead* to watch with me. We were a real family until they started watching shows on the assassination of JFK and the guys that killed him; the murder of Marilyn Monroe; the Mafia controlling the cement industry; separate bedrooms for the royals; sexual harassment in the clergy; sex plagues; living two-headed babies; U.S. military subcultures; meteorite threats to earth; race riots; the complete breakdown of the public-school system; mothers who sell their children; rampant political corruption; cancer from high-voltage lines; father's lover turns out to be wife's long-lost sister; triumph of the drug lords; drunken mortician cremates sleeping janitor by mistake; beauties with biceps; the feminized male; children who divorce their parents; and How Much Loving Do You Really Need?

It was after my parents started watching those kinds of programs that they started going on all their trips and forgetting about me. That was when I set up my first aquarium. I had great guppies, angelfish, and zebra fish. One of the problems with the guppies was that they used to eat their young, but their main problem was when the heating went out in the apartment they froze to death. That was when I got the idea to change the aquarium into a terrarium. I figured I'd have better luck with ferns and moss, but a fungus hit and wiped them out. Then I tried hamsters. They lasted a long time before they kicked the bucket. By then my pal Daniel Barker had socked the bus driver and was shipped off to military school, and I almost had a new friend, Johnny Miller, but his father got laid off and they had to relocate.

It got so all I wanted was some kind of world I could depend on. When nothing really lasted, that was when I saw the notice about the American Cancer Society contest for playwriting. At last I could make up a world, and nobody could take that away from me.

I typed and ate turkey all night. The only break I took was to bring down a thigh and wing for Joe at the door, who was working another double shift. He said it was great and that the cod and striped bass were starting to run off Montauk Point. He also enjoyed telling me again about fishing with his father in Lake Okeechobee.

The next day was Saturday, so I slept for three hours in the morning. I was back at my Smith Corona by noon. I completely rewrote the play. This time I had the character of Al talk right from my heart. For the first time I felt like I was truly putting myself into the script. I gave Al my secret wish, that I could have pals to go to the movies with, and friends to hang out with, a place where friends stayed with me through thick and thin, where no one lied and no one betrayed anybody. I guess I gave my character of Al the curse of a real writer—the curse of wanting what isn't.

I wrote straight through Sunday, when I checked my mother's *Betty Crocker Cookbook* and switched to creamed turkey on points of toast for a change. I could feel all sorts of weird spirits and spooky instincts guiding my writing. Everywhere I turned, I saw visions I put into the play. The morning paper was delivered. Two headlines fit perfectly into the play: ENGLISH TEACHER TERRIFIED WHEN OUIJA BOARD SUMMONS SATAN! and PSYCHIC HEALER TURNS ETHIOPIAN TEENAGER INTO A RODENT!

That night a message from Austria came in on our fax machine:

Dear David,

We're at the Vienna Intercontinental. We dance every night to Strauss waltzes. The wiener schnitzel tastes like butter. How are you? We've changed plans. Now we go to England and fly home Oct. 31 to be with you on Halloween. *The Wall Street Journal* is interested in our doing a feature on a London maxi-mall. We saw a man with one leg dancing. Are you still stooping over? Take extra money from the ATM. Any problems, call Aunt Frieda. Are you still blocked? Dad thinks you should write a sequel to your play on cannibal children. It was excellent. We want you to remember your girl-friend was loony tunes. Don't cry over spilled milk. Drink orange juice. We'll reimburse you when we get home. We'll be at the St. James Hotel, fax 011 44 1 233–8506. Love ya.

Mom and Dad

By midnight I had worked half of my parents' fax into the play. Everything I touched or glimpsed or smelled struck me as important for the character of Al. Clearasil wash. My newly conditioned brown hair. Even Rasputin's groom-ing shears made it in. I was a black hole consum-ing every image I thought of so Al would become a true flesh-and-blood character. At one point I had him break down and admit that he was an emotional cripple.

Monday I was so charged up, I went to school and hardly knew I was there. I kept writing and jotting notes about the play in class. Al had captured my brain. I made low growling animal sounds. First I found myself trying a baboon noise. Then I became a cougar. In English class Miss Conlan asked me how my Meryl Streep vehicle was coming. I mumbled "fine" to her, but a tiny snarl slipped out. I think she thought it was indigestion. After school I went to Woolworth's and picked up three snake plants, two pots of ivy, and six more split-leaf philodendrons on sale. I also found several other discards lying around on curbs for garbage pickup in my neighborhood. Two of the pots had massive stalks, trees with plenty of leaves on them. With a little watering and the sunlight from my terrace, they all started to perk up. The room and I had become completely and utterly alive! By Thursday morning I had finished the rewrite.

Now I deserved to find Della.

First, I thought I should call Bellevue Detox. They wouldn't release information on anybody except to a doctor with a handwritten request. They also wouldn't tell me anything about any "intensive brownstone experiment" on East Twenty-third Street for recovering alcoholics. I called in eight times. The ninth time I spoke to a nurse with a Boston accent. She told me the only volunteer experiment she knew about was for a wrinkle cream and it required that everyone have their nose biopsied twice a week. I figured she didn't know what she was talking about.

I called Actors Equity. They had Della Jones listed as a member.

"We don't give out addresses," a guy in Membership told me. "We do have a contact number I can give you for her, however."

It turned out to be the same number that had been disconnected.

That afternoon I sat with the script on my lap thinking I might have to start walking the streets of Manhattan for the rest of my life to find Della. I put on the TV. Gabrielle Zacks was on doing "The Sassy Edge" news segment of *Teen Time*. The next segment had Ed Weingarten interviewing a club of rap and tap performers. Then he got up and did a nostalgic dance number with them called "Tea For Two," which was so catchy I even played the Caribbean drums along with it. As I clutched the script, I wondered if Della *really* knew him.

That night I wrote a letter to Ed Weingarten. I told him about meeting Della, including everything about me and the play. I explained that Della had said she was his friend. I looked up Ed's cable channel in the phone book. Their offices were on West Fifty-seventh Street, within walking distance from my building.

The next morning I hand-delivered the letter and a copy of the script. The station had a nice receptionist who told me she'd see Ed Weingarten got my package right away.

Now all I could do was wait.

◆◆◆◆◆

They Tore Out My Heart and Stomped That Sucker Flat
——BOOK TITLE BY LEWIS GRIZZARD

There is no gravity. It's just that the earth sucks.
——WRITTEN ON A BATHROOM WALL

◆◆◆◆◆

9

◆◆◆◆◆

Early Saturday morning my phone rang. I
leaned across my bed and answered it.

"Hello?"

"David Mahooley?"

"Yes. Who's this?"

"Ed Weingarten."

"Really?"

"Of course, really. It's not the kind of thing
anyone would make up, I don't think. I got your
letter and script. I'd like to get together with
you and talk about it. You're over at Thirty-two
Lincoln Plaza?"

"Yes." My throat began to close. I'd never
thought a celebrity kid with his own TV show

would actually take the time to call me. "When?"

"What's your schedule today?"

"Nothing."

"I've got a brunch at ten fifteen and a London call at eleven. I could stop over around noon."

"Today?"

"Yeah. Okay?"

"Sure."

"Great."

"Did you like my play?"

"Well, I want to talk to you about it," he said. "And Della. I'll tell you when I see you."

"Okay."

He hung up.

I broke out in a cold sweat. Ed Weingarten had actually read my play and was coming over! I remembered Della saying Ed's main problem in life was that he and Gabrielle had gotten into some social-political experiment that was freaky and bizarre. Anything "freaky and bizarre" to Della would have to be mind-boggling.

I took a shower and put Miracle Grow on all the terrace plants, the philodendrons in my room, and the Chia pet on my desk. By eleven thirty I had so much caffeine and adrenalin pumping through my veins, I had to pace out on my terrace. I could see everyone below coming in and out of the building.

The morning paper was filled with omens. The lead story in the Metro Section was that the Wind Song Sushi Bar was closed down by the Board of Health because of the way the restaurant drained water from cabbages. It said they put their cabbages in cloth laundry bags, placed them between two pieces of plywood in their parking lot and drove over them with a Toyota 4x4. The story right next to it reported that jail officials in Winnipeg, Canada, had turned down inmate Morgan Kreig's request to keep a *Webster's Collegiate Dictionary* in his cell, saying it could be used as a weapon.

The barking from the hydroponic's terrace became so bad by a quarter to twelve, I barked back at them. I got the dogs so rabid they began chewing their terrace railing. Eventually, I saw the bathrobe hem of their phantom owner as he swooped out, let them inside, and turned up the mist on me.

At noon I looked down from my terrace and saw a tall teenage girl with a short boy come down the street. They stopped under the awning of my building. A moment later the boy turned around and headed back up Broadway. The tall girl walked into the building.

The intercom buzzed.

"Yes Joe?"

"Miss Weingarten's here."

"Miss?"

"Yeah."

"Send her up." I had no idea who *Miss* Weingarten was. Maybe she was Ed's sister and she was meeting him here too. Who knew?

The door chimes sounded.

I opened the door.

There stood a tall blond girl with Ed Weingarten's face.

"You're David?"

"Yes."

"I'm Ed."

I looked closer and I could see it *was* Ed Weingarten dressed as a very trendy teenage girl. For a moment I thought I was losing my mind. He was juggling my script in his hands.

I cleared my throat.

"Nice to meet you," I said.

I couldn't take my eyes off his big jaw and shoulder length straight hair, all the features I recognized from TV. He was immaculately dressed in a black skirt and jacket and wearing high-heeled patent leather shoes. He looked a lot like Jodie Foster.

"May I come in?" he asked, flipping his hair.

"Yes, of course," I said quickly.

I ushered him into the living room. I guess he noticed the look on my face.

"Della told you about the gender-bending project Gabrielle and I are into?"

"She only told me you were doing some kind of social-political experiment," I answered, trying to sound like we were just talking about the weather. He walked toward the big stainless-steel coffee table in the living room and sat on the sofa.

"You want a Coke or a Yoo-Hoo?" I asked.

"No thanks." He crossed his legs. His left shiny shoe tip bobbed in front of him like a hammer driving in a nail. I mean, he wasn't trying to act feminine or anything like that. Everything about him was very masculine except his skirt and makeup.

"I need a glass of water," I said, excusing myself and heading for the kitchen. I was dying of curiosity, so I called over my shoulder, "I was looking off the balcony and saw you were with a *boy*."

"Yeah, that's Gabrielle," he called in to me. "We had to cross-dress today because we've got an Anti-Defamation League luncheon at the Tavern on the Green."

"Why?" I asked.

He laughed. "It's part of our experiment—but she thought she'd just stop over at Tower Records first to pick up a Red Hot Chili Peppers album. She'll stop back for me."

I chugalugged my glass of water and stumbled back to the living room. I sat across from him. His shoe tip still bobbed.

"You look freaked out," he said.

"Huh?" I thought I was hearing things.

"Your eyes are bulging out of your skull."

"I'm sorry," I said.

"Hey, don't let it throw you because I'm dressed a little differently," he said, trying to calm me.

"You're dressed more than a little differently, wouldn't you say?" I finally had to let him know.

He looked offended. "One thing we'd better get straight right from the top," he said gruffly, "is I'm not here because I'm knocked out by you or your play."

"I didn't mean to insult you."

"I only came over because you're messing with Della, and she's one of the greatest talents Gabrielle and I know."

"Look," I said, "I care for her a lot too."

He still looked and sounded ticked off. "Even on the slim chance I were to produce your play, you'd better know a little more about how I work."

"I'd like a few clues," I said, trying to sound as sincere as possible.

He finally relaxed back in his seat. "I don't pick a play to produce unless I'm connected to it," he said, toying with one of his earrings. "Any producer—the Shuberts or Nederlanders, anyone at the Kennedy Center—we all pick a play that touches our own lives. If your play was about Carmelite nuns, the only kind of producer who'd go for it would be one who had a sister or an aunt who was a Carmelite nun. You get what I'm saying about connecting?"

He had a boy-do-you-look-stupid expression on his face that made me want to punch him in the nose.

"I only wrote you because I need to get in touch with Della," I said.

"And you just happened to include a copy of your script."

"So?"

He leaned forward. His hair all flowed to the front strand by strand like a Slinky. *"How do I know if you're normal, that you're not some kind of nut?"* he asked.

"You're sitting there in a skirt with blue eyeliner and want to know if *I'm* normal?"

"You don't realize what an amazing creature Della is, do you?"

"I don't think *you* do," I had to tell him.

"Della brought out a special chemistry between Gabrielle and me."

"Oh, I'm sure it's special," I agreed.

"We're into a truth that's way beyond you, pal," he said. "Our whole idea to gender bend is a way of jolting a little reality into our society. It came out of a Westinghouse Science Scholarship we were going for at our high school. We figured what the world didn't need was another potato clock! Gabrielle and I wanted to do something really different. We're not gay. We just wanted to test the limits on this whole gender bending that's going on. Our whole society's into it. It's multipierced ears and pony tails for the guys and tattoos and men's suit jackets for the girls. And that's cool with us, except we noticed boys and girls sort of not trusting or *liking* each other very much anymore."

"Who says?" I insisted on knowing.

He recrossed his legs again, and leaned back. Now his other foot bobbed as his hair slinked into a new position.

"Look, Gabrielle and I know we're pushing the envelope. I mean, we don't flaunt it on our TV show, but we needed to make a loud statement about what was happening. We cross-dress in public so we can illuminate the really deep trouble American society is in. Gabrielle and I were inspired by a lecture by Dr. Norman Reese at the New York Philosophic Society where he presented proof positive that four thousand years ago the entire population of Dijon, France—where they make the mustard—had a sexual split, a type of living Hegelian dialectic, as Dr. Reese called it, in which the guys and girls grew to hate each other so much that the guys all moved underground and lived in caves, while the girls lived on the surface—for a very long time—until their hatred grew so strong that one morning the guys rose up from beneath the earth, and they and the girls tried to club each other to death. Needless to say, Gabrielle and I are committed to not letting history repeat itself. That's why the libbers, the Young Republicans clubs, the metaphysical and equality groups, they all want to know what Gabrielle and I have to report from the field. We put out an apocalyptic monthly newsletter called *The Last Date*." He stood up, straightened his skirt, and walked to the living room windows. "What this all bottom lines to from your point of view is *Della*. Before I tell you where to find her, I need to be certain you're not part of this festering hate movement. Della couldn't live through another sicko."

"You're talking about Al?" I asked.

"Yeah."

"She wouldn't tell me how it ended. What did he do to her?" I needed to know.

"Whatever it was," he said sadly, "she started drinking. We know he took one of the most gentle and talented girls Gabrielle and I ever knew and really messed her up. I need to know up front what you feel for Della."

"I'm not sure I should tell you," I said nervously.

"Hey, relax, buddy. I like your play. Gabrielle does too. We want to produce it with Della starring in it."

I sat forward in my seat. *"You do?"*

"It'll be a full off-Broadway production. Gabrielle's uncle's got the bucks; he's networked with a lot of backers. You'll make money out of it. Full legal contracts, the whole scene. More importantly, Della will make some money too."

"She needs it more than I do," I said.

He walked toward me. "For me"—he sighed—"well, I can't be the Peter Pan host of *Teen Talk* forever. I need a solid theater credit. That's the story." He sat in the chair next to mine. "Now I ask you again, what do you feel for Della?"

I felt like I was on the spot. I didn't know why, but I believed everything Ed Weingarten said. He looked crazy in a girl's dress, but he was the sharpest kid I'd ever talked to. I believed he would produce my play, but I also knew he would know if I lied.

"I mean," Ed continued, "how do you love her? Do you love her like yourself? Do you love her like your father or mother? What is she to you? A pal? Venus? A sister? Are you a teenage transference freak? I've got to get a handle on how you love her so you don't send Della's life further down the toilet than Al did."

"I feel for Della like an eel," I said.

Now Ed's eyeballs bulged. *"Like an eel?"*

"I love her like an eel."

"I don't understand," he said.

"It's just that I had to do a lot of research on animals," I admitted. "I had to think a lot about Al and his thing for fauna. I never really got attached to anything from a jungle like I guess he did. Not really. But when I was trying to write his character and understand him, I read about eels, and when I did, I knew I wanted my love with Della to be like that. Like with eels."

"How is it with eels?"

My voice fell to a whisper. What I had to tell him was very personal. "All eels in the whole world are born in one place, in a seaweed bed south of Bermuda called the Sargasso Sea," I said. "And from the Sargasso Sea, the American eels swim to Canada and New England. Some of them have to swim for as long as four years, the boy and girl eels swimming next to each other, until they arrive at the mouth of their particular river. Just imagine, one boy and one girl eel arriving at the mouth of the Delaware. And, for some reason no one knows, there the boy and girl eels separate. The boy stays near the river mouth, but the girl swims up the river without him. She swims for many, many miles far up the river until she reaches a pond that is meant for her."

Ed leaned forward and looked really interested. "It's like the boy eel gets Cape May and the girl eel ends up in Port Jervis?"

"Exactly," I said. "She lives without the boy for over ten years, settling into the pond and learning whatever it is girl eels have to learn. Meanwhile, the boy eel waits in the saltwater at the river's mouth, learning what he must in the sea. And then a day comes when the girl eel knows it is time to swim back to the sea. She heads back the way she came, swimming in terrifying river currents, crashing down waterfalls, and being hurled against rocks. Sometimes she's forced to leave the water altogether to crawl along great stretches of mud and land, and then back into the water. Finally, she makes it to the river mouth, where the boy eel waits for her. He knows she's coming. He's there and greets her, and together they swim all the way back to the Sargasso Sea. There, in that place, in the same seaweed beds where they were born, they mate and spawn and live and finally die together. That's the kind of love I feel for Della."

"That's very, very beautiful," Ed said. "I hear what you're saying."

The intercom buzzed.

"That's Gabrielle," Ed said, checking his watch. "We've got to get over to the luncheon. Say I'll be right down."

I pressed the intercom button.

"What, Joe?"

"A young man's down here for Miss Weingarten."

"Tell him she'll be right down."

I turned to face Ed. He handed me a slip of paper.

"Here's Della's address. It's her mother's apartment in Chinatown. They live over a squid-and-barbecued-duck restaurant. I'll call you tonight. There's a few other things you'll need to know."

"Like what?"

He straightened his skirt as I walked him to

the door. "Della's worked a lot. Commercials as a kid. A lot of theater, some TV. Every casting director in New York got to know her early on. They knew she was the biggest talent coming down the pike in a decade. But they all know her M.O. by now."

"Her *what*?"

"The way she operates," he said, opening the front door.

I walked out with him to the elevator and pressed the button.

"Ever since Al, since the drinking, she's been hired for a lot of things, even dinner theater. She shows up for rehearsals to get paid, but quits before the play opens. She ties a big load on, and bolts before an audience is able to see her. The more truth in a play, the more she's going to bolt. She'll try to run out on us and sink the production. That's just the way she is, and you have to be the one to change that."

"I will."

The elevator came. He got in but held the door from closing.

"I really believe you're going to try. Della's beautiful and talented and a fantastic trip. She's also very scary."

"I'll do what I have to do."

"You going to try to find her today?"

"Yes."

"Gabrielle and I will say a prayer for you," he said, shaking my hand. "Della probably didn't get around to telling you we're Seventh Day Adventists, also."

"No, she didn't."

He let the elevator door close.

I walked back up the hall, went into the apartment, and closed the door. I looked down at the writing on the piece of paper in my hand. "161 1/2 Mott Street. Be careful."

◆◆◆◆◆

Love is the crocodile on the river of desire.
——BHARTRHARI (A.D. 625)

Schizophrenia beats dining alone.
——UNKNOWN

10

I needed a plan. If only Daniel Barker wasn't in Vancouver, or if I had any friend I could call. Even if Rasputin were still alive, I'd have given him a bath and talked everything over with him. It wouldn't have mattered that he was a dog. He was a really good, sympathetic listener. The problem with Della was out of Joe's league—he was a lot better on bluefish feeding patterns than teenage dipsomania. Della had problems I'd have to help her deal with as best I could. If I didn't, I'd be doing exactly what I had done with Kim. I'd be an ostrich with my head in the sand.

I wanted to get Della out of Chinatown and

back up to my apartment. I wanted her to see how I'd made my room into a special garden for both of us.

I went to Woolworth's and bought seventeen dollars' worth of ivy, gloxinias, and mums. I made a fresh copy of the script. I also picked up a major lock for my parents' liquor cabinet from Kinski's Hardware store.

By the time the six-P.M. TV news came on, my room looked like a set for a Tarzan movie. What I liked best was the way I'd arranged two big pots of vines in each of the dummy's arms so it looked like a statue guarding an ancient Yucatan temple. I took Polaroid shots of everything in case Della needed proof that my room and I were seething with life. She'd see the plants, my brimming Clothesline of Plot, the Post-It notes all around my desk.

I was dressed and ready to walk out the door when the phone rang.

"Hello?"

"Hi. It's me, Ed."

"I'm just heading down to Chinatown now," I said. "I want to bring Della back up here."

"Listen, Gabrielle and I decided we want to see her too. We've got a Daughters of the American Revolution dinner tonight. We'll stop by after, if you think it's okay."

"Sure."

"Good luck!" he said, and hung up.

The fax machine was directly in front of me. In all the times my parents had taken off and left me, I'd never sent them a fax. Tonight would be different. No more being an ostrich with its head in the sand with *them* either. It was about time I let them know a thing or two I really felt in my heart. My message was simple and came easily. It was one I should have sent a long time ago:

Dear Mom and Dad,

I know you won't get this until you reach the St. James Hotel in London. I should have sent it to Tasmania, New Zealand, Club Med, and a lot of other places years ago. I think you need to know I don't like you both running off and leaving me alone all the time. In Vienna you said you saw a man with one leg dancing. Did you ever happen to notice I've been trying to dance with one leg? Mom and Dad, I can't get everything from an automatic teller machine. And I hate Aunt Frieda. She's a cruel, sadistic storm trooper. I'd like to shove her rice pudding down her throat and lock her down in her cellar with the spiders. You both are never there for me anymore. Kim was a human being. You could have helped me understand the kind of mental problem she had. You could have both helped me deal with a lot of problems I've had growing up, instead of the two of you farting around on camels. Mom and Dad, you've neglected me and I feel rotten about it. What can't you stand about me? Why are you both so selfish? Why do you run away? No, you can't reimburse me when you come home. You used to be excited that you had a son. Now you're more excited if you've had wiener schnitzel or goulash! Mom and Dad, I protest! I'm furious! I'm not going to put up with it! Don't bother faxing me anymore. Why aren't you here for me to talk to? Didn't you ever notice I've lost every friend and pal I ever had? Couldn't you have helped me? Why aren't you here even when you're here?

Sincerely yours,
David

I caught a subway at Columbus Circle. I took it all the way downtown to Canal Street. A full, big, orange moon hung low in the sky, so I decided to walk the rest of the way. I passed six or seven Army and Navy supply stores. There was a big, bustling kosher dairy restaurant, and then a whole block of gyro-souvlaki sandwich stands. Past Broadway it got Chinese very quickly. There were culinary sights that could've knocked off the appetite of the entire Donner party. Trucks filled with stiff, white pig carcasses. Fish stores with guys chopping heads off like it was fun.

The worst thing I saw was a market with big goldfish trying to swim in a shallow tub with their backs half sticking up out of the water. This guy was taking out one at a time and socking it with a cleaver. Then came a string of ginseng stores with roots shaped like human embryos standing upright in glass bottles. My vote for the top upchuck vision of the night was a basket of tasty treasures under a sign that said, SALE—39 CENTS A POUND—ROAST PIG LIPS AND DUCK HEADS.

When I reached Mott Street I turned north. One sixty-one and a half was smack above a busy restaurant called the Nam Wah Pan. Through the front window I could see lots of people slurping squid and really weird-looking stuff.

I walked up a rickety stairway on the side to an apartment door. The black paint on the door was peeling. The whole building looked like a dump.

The name JONES was scrawled above the buzzer. I felt sorry for Della and her mother. The idea of raising a baby in a place like that was really spooky. I pressed the buzzer.

No one answered.

I gave a loud knock on the door.

The apartment windows were covered with soot. Dark, ripped curtains hung in the windows. There was no way I could tell if anyone was peeking out at me.

I knocked again.

Finally, there were metal clicking sounds from the other side of the door. The door opened as far as three chain locks would allow. A slab of a woman's face stared out at me from the slit.

"Whaddya want?"

I looked into bloodshot eyes lurking behind strands of limp brown hair.

"Are you Della's mother? Are you the poet?"

She glared at me. "Who are you?"

"I'm David Mahooley, Mrs. Jones. I'm a friend." I tried to flash my best idiotic, harmless grin. "I wrote a play for Della. Didn't she tell you?"

"She doesn't tell me diddily-squat." She gave me a little wink. "She's not here, you know. She's got a job."

"A job?"

"Yes."

I didn't hear any sounds from the baby daughter Della had said she had. I figured it was probably sleeping. Mrs. Jones lifted a hand up between the chain locks and pointed left up the street. "She's working around the corner. Gum Sum's liquor store. She's there now, if you wanna see her."

"Thanks."

"Hey, did you know that Andrew Jackson sold slaves? Did you know that?" she asked, right out of the blue.

"No, I didn't."

"He *did*." She laughed and closed the door.

I retreated down the shaky stairs. I walked up the street by a Chinese bakery and an herb shop. I didn't like the idea of Della working in a liquor store.

Gum Sum's was the weirdest-shaped store I'd ever seen. It was only as wide as an alley, but very long. On closer inspection, I could tell it actually *had* once been an alley between two buildings, and then was closed in. Above the GUM SUM LIQUORS orange neon sign was a pair of big speakers blasting Chinese rock 'n' roll music out onto the street. I bumped into a dozen people making my way into the store. A cashier sat on a high ladder watching for shoplifters.

"I'm looking for Della Jones," I said to him.

He answered in Chinese, pointing over the mob of customers' heads. I squeezed deeper into the store with my hand on my money in case there were any pickpockets working the crowd. A few feet farther I spotted an explosion of curly hair trickling down onto a long, crushed-velvet dress. I saw Della's lovely face. Her neck was speckled with reflections from a crystal necklace. She saw me.

"What're you doing here?"

"I finished the play," I shouted over the pounding music.

"Good."

"And I've got a producer."

Della's eyes lit up.

"Who?"

"Can we go talk?"

"Who's the producer?"

"The Shuberts and Nederlanders were mentioned. And the Kennedy Center." I wasn't lying. Ed Weingarten *had* mentioned them.

"The Kennedy Center?"

Her mascara-laden eyes opened wide, then narrowed. I knew I might have gone too far.

"Not that the play's right for the Kennedy Center," I added quickly, "but the least it'll end up with is a full off-Broadway production. You'll make money."

"How'd you find me?"

"Your mother."

A flash of terror crossed her face.

"You went to my mother's apartment?"

"I didn't go in. I was hoping you'd be there. I wanted to see your daughter, too."

"My baby goes to sleep early. How'd you get the address?"

"A friend at Actors Equity gave it to me as a favor," I lied.

"You didn't go *in* the apartment?"

"No."

I could see she was relieved.

"Did my mother talk your ear off about Andrew Jackson?"

"Not much."

"Good." She noticed the envelope in my hand. "Is that the script?"

"Yes."

"When would we start rehearsals?"

"Soon."

"I want to read the script first."

"Can you get out of here? We could go up to my apartment; you can read the play."

"I'll meet you out front." She turned on her heels and headed for the back room of the store.

I fought my way out the way I'd come in. Finally, I was back outside on the sidewalk. The speakers still blasted away with Chinese rock 'n' roll.

Della came out lugging her old gym bag. It looked heavier than ever.

"I'll carry it," I offered.

"No, I can handle it."

She hurried through the crowds with me trailing after her. Ahead, beyond Chinatown, were the lights of an Italian street festival.

"What about your baby?"

"She sleeps through the night. My mother's actually very good with her. I can't wait to read your script!"

She turned into the doorway of the Bella Luna Cafe.

"Hey, where are you going?"

"We need a drink!" she laughed, taking my arm. "Just a little celebration drink!"

◆◆◆◆◆

Writers aren't exactly people . . . they're a whole lot of people trying to be one person.
                                        —F. SCOTT FITZGERALD

There's a great woman behind every idiot.
                                        —JOHN LENNON ON YOKO ONO

11

Della scooted to a table against a wall that was painted with a huge map of Italy. She sat down, snapped her fingers for a waiter, and ordered a white wine before I even got into my seat. There was such a sophisticated way she had of doing everything, she came off looking a lot older than she was. Nobody asked for her I.D. She started reading the script by the light from a big dripping candle on the table.

"Whadda you havin'?" the waiter asked me.

"You have cannolis?"

"Of course we have cannolis."

"I want one."

"Chocolate covered?"

"No."

"Whadda you want to drink?"

"A cappuccino."

He headed for the bar and a long refrigerator display case filled with desserts. Della's eyes scanned my pages like lasers.

"You're not supposed to drink wine, are you?"

"Everything's cool," she said, without even looking up. "I passed the Brownstone Experiment with flying colors."

"I thought if you were alcoholic you had to give up booze for the rest of your life."

"I was never a real alcoholic."

The waiter came back with our order. By the time I finished my cannoli and cappuccino, Della had moved on to a second glass of wine.

"What do you think of the play so far?"

"Not bad."

By page thirty-eight she had laughed out loud twice.

"It's good to have a little humor, don't you think?"

"Sure. Let's get out of here."

I paid the bill. We went back out to Delancey Street. "We can cab it right up to my apartment."

"Not yet." She headed us west to the SoHo Bar & Grill. She had a glass of sherry there, and read fifteen more pages. After that it was the El Sombrero Inn on Bleecker Street. She read another couple dozen pages and polished off a water glass of wine there. I stuck with Diet Coke. I decided I'd better show her the Polaroid shots of all the plants before she got too plastered to see them.

"Oh David," she gasped, looking at the photos, "is this your room? Is it really your room?"

"Yes."

"Oh God, it's a forest! You've turned your entire room into a forest!"

"Mites tried to take over the ivy, but I knocked them off with a d-Con pesticide spray!"

"It looks crazy, David! I love it! I love it! I've got to see it!"

"Yes!"

"I can't wait."

That's all I was waiting for. "Let's go!" I said, signaling the waiter for the check.

Outside, I managed to hail a cab at the corner of Seventh Avenue. Della laughed, clutching my script in one hand and her gym bag in the other. The driver turned out to be some kind of maniac with a temporary operator's permit. At least we were heading uptown. Della kept reading the script in the cab.

"I couldn't stop collecting plants until I finished the writing," I said.

"You've made a beautiful jungle!" she said, without lifting her eyes from the script.

"You think so?"

"Yes!"

The cab shot uptown like a rocket. The driver swerved, ran through changing lights, and charged across double and triple lanes of traffic without blinking an eye. All Della did was laugh and keep turning pages. We made it to the corner of Broadway and Sixty-third Street alive. While I paid the fare, Della leaped out singing, "Dee dum da dee dum." That was fine, but she didn't head for the entrance to my building. She dashed into the Rolling Stone Saloon next door. The place was packed and jumping, but I caught up with her at the bar. She'd already ordered a drink called a "horse's neck."

"Hey, Della, I want to show you my room."

"Yeah, right after this." She giggled, chewing on a piece of orange rind.

Most of the waiters and waitresses were on

roller skates, and there was a big crowd dancing to a small country-western band they always have there.

Two horse's necks later, Della had finished the script.

"So, what do you think?" I asked.

"It's brilliant! I'm knocked out by it."

"I got possessed."

"We need to dance," she cried out, dragging me onto the dance floor. We started doing a fast two-step like everyone else.

"You really came through for us, David! You really did!"

"You think the play's brilliant? You really do?"

"It's profound and touching and charming and very, very *real*! It's everything I could have dreamed of!" She started to spin. Her hair hit one of the waiters and almost knocked him off his roller skates. I was so thrilled she loved the play, I actually found myself enjoying the dancing.

"You are such a cutie," she said. "You really are!"

"Then you'll do my play?"

"Of course I will. I'll do it for you, and for me and my baby daughter! I'll do it for the world!"

she shouted above the band.

"You never told me your baby's name."

"Oh, it's Tiara. I think it's nice to have a unique first name, so if you ever become a star in Las Vegas all they have to put in the ads are things like 'TIARA'S AT THE MIRAGE!' or 'TIARA'S AT THE EXCALIBUR!'"

"Tiara is a beautiful name. And you're sure you're okay with that Brownstone Experiment, that they taught you how to control everything or whatever you're supposed to do?"

"No sweat. Look, I'm very touched that you care about me. And I'm very moved that you brought me your play, that you didn't forget about me when you found a producer. I'm going to make you very proud. You did it! You rang the bell with this play! It's going to be a winner. Ding dong, ding dong!"

"I even started composing a solo on the Caribbean drums, just a little one for the play."

"You're putting a Caribbean drum solo into the play?"

"Just like a preshow thing, or maybe for intermission."

"Sure, what's an intermission without a drum solo!"

"And the climax is great, right?"

"Incredible."

"I thought it was mystical. Even when I was writing the stage directions, I couldn't stop myself from being creative. Did you notice the stage directions? Did you?"

"How could I miss the one at the end of Act I, where you say 'Al exits like a punctured balloon'!"

"Do you realize you've become my greatest fiction?"

"That's very sweet," Della said. The band stopped playing, and she led me back to the bar. She slugged back the rest of her horse's neck. "Now tell me about the producer. Who's producing?"

"We've got a lot of business to talk about," I said, paying the check. This time I didn't ask her, I just told her we were going up to my apartment. I went to grab her gym bag, but she beat me to it. She was feeling so good, she blew kisses to half the waiters and the band as we went out the door. She was still dancing a jig on the sidewalk. Some people coming out of a foreign film at the cineplex stared, but finally we made it into my building.

"Hi, David," Joe said, as we burst into the lobby.

"Hi," I said.

"Hi Joe! Hi Joe," Della sang out to him, and started spinning under the center chandelier. "Oh, look at all the *lights*!"

"I got a great catch of mackerel out at Sheepshead Bay yesterday," Joe said.

"Nice," I said.

I got Della into the elevator fast. "Congratulations on all your mackerels!" she called out before the door closed.

We got off at my floor. I took the key out of my pocket and opened the door to the apartment. I told Della to wait a minute while I ran around putting on lights, but she barged right into the kitchen and pulled a bottle of Spanish wine out of her gym bag.

"You got a corkscrew?"

"In the drawer next to the sink," I said. "A glass is in the cabinet over the counter."

I dashed down to my room, turned two of the ceiling track-light units smack on the ivy-laden dummy, and put the terrace lights on so the philodendrons and potted trees would be silhouetted. Della sang as she headed down the hall, "Love is la dee, dum da dee dee, la dum dee . . ." I'd never heard her sound happier.

"In *here*!"

Della danced into my room clutching her drink in one hand and her gym bag in the other. She set her bag down and whirled like a dervish. "It's even more spectacular than in the photos!"

"Last week I started feeding them a Burpee fertilizer solution. I noticed the hydroponic freak is always getting packages from Burpee. They just lie around downstairs in the mailroom off the lobby."

"Hello, plants! Hello, darlings!" Della threw open the terrace door. "Hello, Mr. Hydroponics!" she called up to his terrace, and laughed.

"Joe told me the hydroponic guy's grown a three-hundred-pound pumpkin now."

"Live and let live," Della cried out. She dashed to my desk and sat in my swivel chair. She began spinning as fast as she could. Then she remembered something and stopped the chair dead.

"All right, who's the producer?"

"The producer?" I hesitated again.

"Yes, who is it? What's his name?"

"You want to know his name?"

Her brow wrinkled and her eyes narrowed. "Yes."

"Exactly?"

"Yes, of course *exactly*." Her voice climbed a few decibels.

"Ed Weingarten."

"Ed Weingarten?" she repeated quizzically.

"Yes."

"Is this your idea of a little joke?" She laughed hollowly; her eyes zapped right onto my face. "Come on, now, who's *really* producing?"

"Ed Weingarten," I repeated. She started to breathe heavily, and pulled back away from me like a snake coiling. "I didn't want to tell you at first, because I figured you'd be a little upset," I confessed.

She began to shake. "Are you out of your mind?"

"No, see, Actors Equity and Bellevue Detox wouldn't give me your address, so I remembered you saying you were such a good friend of Ed Weingarten's. I contacted him and he was thrilled to hear about you and my play. He loves you and the script!"

Della stood up clenching her fists. "You called Ed Weingarten?" She looked very, very disturbed.

"Yes," I admitted.

"*Are you out of your mind?*" she screamed at me.

"I'm not out of my mind," I said, offended. "He and Gabrielle love you. He's going to make a great producer on this."

"You're trying to tell me that you came all the way down to Chinatown"—she huffed—"gave me a song and dance about us going into rehearsal soon, that you had the whole play package together? We just had to take a few meetings and it'd be a 'GO' project! We'd start rehearsals, like in a week or something? You've dragged me up here by mentioning all those big names, and the producer turns out to be Ed Weingarten?" She started to *really* scream. "ED WEINGARTEN IS MY FRIEND. HE IS MY PERSONAL FRIEND AND YOU HAD NO RIGHT TO GO TO HIM! NO RIGHT AT ALL! AND HE IS A TERRIBLE PRODUCER!"

"Hey, we're not talking *Mermaids Off Wee-hawken* with this play."

"His mind is on social causes!"

"I know. He came over here in pearls and high heels."

"Ed Weingarten came to this apartment?" She grabbed her drink and began to pace in circles.

"Hey, Ed's going to make this happen!" She suddenly tripped on her gym bag. There was a racket of bottles hitting each other. She looked horrified as she stooped to open the bag. I couldn't help seeing she had five bottles of vodka and a quart of gin. "Why do you have so much booze?"

"You told me you had major backing!" she yelled, rearranging the bottles in her gym bag as if they were her babies.

"Ed's got it all worked out."

"He's got nothing worked out."

"He'll tell you himself. He said he and Gabrielle would stop over after their dinner."

"Ed Weingarten's coming here?"

"Yes, they're at some kind of charity event. Look, Ed's got savvy. He cares about you. He knows you need money. Gabrielle's uncle's going to guarantee the money. They'll work out a union budget for the show and everything. I know he'll keep the budget down so the play can have a long run and you'll get a salary, Della. A good salary! Just think, a full off-Broadway production! He believes in you."

"I don't work for minimum, you know."

I put my hand on her shoulder and said what I

had to say. "Don't worry. Ed knows your whole M.O."

"What do you mean he knows my whole M.O.?"

I picked up her gym bag of booze.

"What are you doing?"

I didn't say a word, but turned quickly and hurried down the hall to my father's liquor cabinet. I stuck her bag inside the closet, closed the door, and locked it. I put the key deep in my right pants pocket. In a flash, Della was right behind me, braying at my neck.

"How dare you lock up my liquor?" She started to pull on the door, and then bang on it.

"Della, lay off the alcohol. Ed told me all about your routine, and we've got to help you break it."

I headed back to my room, but she beat me there, grabbing her half-full glass before I could get my hands on it. "Ed's really looking forward to seeing you."

"But I don't want to see Ed Weingarten!"

"He knows you only agree to be in a play to get advances and rehearsal pay." I knew I'd have to talk straight if I was going to stand a chance with her, so I threw in a few thoughts of my own, too. "The only reason you came here tonight was to see how soon you could be getting a salary advance, and then you'd do as you usually do: tie one big load on and make sure you're fired or quit before an audience might actually see our play. Look, Della, Ed put me onto all those destructive things you do. He really loves you. He and Gabrielle both know what it takes for you to go out in front of an audience. They really want to help you make it this time!"

She slugged down the last of the booze in her glass. "What makes Ed or Gabrielle or you think this time would be any different?"

"He made me promise to baby-sit you through opening night," I invented. "If we can get you to open to an audience cold sober, I think you'll be all right."

"Oh, wait a minute, nobody baby-sits me."

"I guess we'd better get it all out. I baby-sit you or you don't do my play. I'm telling you, no holds barred, that's the bottom line. I may not have a lot of professional experience, but I'm not going to let you sink me and my play—and yourself! Your drinking stops now! It stops right this minute." I went to put my arm around her, but she slapped it away. "Della, let me help you."

"Just who do you think you are?"

"Della, I love you very much."

She looked frightened to death. "Look, let me save us both a lot of anguish, and I'll leave quietly. Let's just say things didn't work out. Let's be kind and chalk it up to artistic differences."

She headed toward the door of my room, but I ran in front of her and slammed it shut. I put my back against it. "Don't leave, Della. Please don't."

"I want out of here before Ed Weingarten shows up in an evening dress," she said.

"Della, I know why you're terrified. I know it's more than your drinking problem. Ed told me the greater the truth in a play, the more frightened you get and the more you want to bolt."

"Let's just make believe you never said that."

"You'd be stupid to walk out on this part."

She laughed right in my face.

"You said the play was brilliant," I reminded her.

"Yeah, but what I said and what *is* are two different things."

"Come on, Della, at least be fair. You're not going to say there's something wrong with my play?"

"Let's just say if it would emphasize that point, I'd spin my head around seven times and upchuck in pentameter."

"My play probably is too poetic for you."

"The only poetry it reminds me of is something the poet Robert Burns said about a piece of writing of equal quality. He said, 'Thou eunuch of language, thou pimp of gender and pickle-herring in a puppet show of nonsense.'"

"That's low. That's really low."

She turned away from me and the door and began pacing in a circle again. "There's still no sensitive, caring boy in your play. Your Al is still a cold fish because he's *you*!"

"I'll do a little rewriting in rehearsal."

"Rewriting? Don't you know how it's all supposed to work? See, a writer's supposed to live a little and get a little wounded. And then he's supposed to create something as compensation for what he's missing—and in spots, you know, you could be a little weird. I mean, as a writer you're supposed to take all that baggage you've got and be compelling and truthful and daring and even vulgar. And you can even be fed by the memory of that pathetic creature you called your girlfriend or me or whatever pain you want to dredge up! And, in case you didn't know it, you're supposed to do all that and shove it through a prism until it screams out like a burning light to touch every little troubled human on this sad planet. So let's be nice about it and just say you failed! You failed! You failed!"

"You think I don't feel? You think I have no feelings?"

"Yeah. Take *'don't feel'* and shove it under an electron microscope and then look at it, and you'll see how much you and that block of wood you wrote doesn't feel. I'd better go, because if Ed Weingarten walked in right this minute in high heels, I'd choke him!" she said.

"I gave Al everything I felt."

She walked to face me at the door.

"Let's not do this. After all, what do I know? Please step aside and I'll see you around sometime."

"Don't go. I wrote this one from my heart! I need to know what's wrong with my heart!"

"Just forget everything I said. You and Ed get yourself another actress, and I'll send a singing telegram to you all on opening night. Now get out of my way."

"No."

She grabbed me and started to pull me away from the door. I refused to budge, but she tricked me by faking to my left and then shooting around my right. Before I knew what had happened, she was behind me, shoving me right at my bed. I was off balance and fell forward onto it.

"I could've just given you one good uppercut and stepped over your body," she said.

I moved up into a sitting position. "Let me talk to you; at least let me talk."

"Then talk faster, because I can't listen so slowly! You're so stupid."

"You think you're the first one to call me stupid?"

"No. I think they line up to call you stupid."

"Della, you can't just shoot in here a couple of times like you're on Rollerblades and think everything's going to be perfect. Real love between a boy and a girl takes a little time. Feelings for a boy and a girl need some kind of history. The only frame of reference you have for a great love relationship is some boy who made out with you like a bat! Sure, I'm a little more conventional, but at least I won't give you rabies. I've done the best I can to make us come alive in my play and in real life. Why can't you see my Al in the play? The boy I wrote is me, and he loves you. You've got to meet me halfway. I am Al in the play. I don't fall in love fast, but when I do, I hang on like a bull-dog. With me it'd be forever."

"I need a drink."

"You don't need a drink."

"Look, David, there is no way I could play any girl who falls in love anymore. Not ever. I don't believe in love anymore. It just doesn't happen."

"Yes it does."

"Oh, it happens, maybe, but no one wants to know the truth about it. At least no boy or girl I ever met wanted to know what love really is."

"You think you know?"

"Yes."

The phone rang and I grabbed it.

"Hi, David." I heard Ed's voice.

"Oh, hi, Ed. Yes, Della's here. You want to talk to her?"

Della frowned and shook her head.

"I mean, she can't come to the phone right

now." A word to the wise was enough for Ed. "Okay, I'll tell her." I hung up.

"Ed said he and Gabrielle were on dessert. They'll be over in forty-five minutes."

"Good," Della said. "I'll be history by then."

"Della, what you think is love, this awful thing that you think it is, has something to do with the 'irregular' way you and Al ended everything, doesn't it? It has to do with something even more irregular than him thinking he was a member of Mensa from another planet, doesn't it?"

"You don't want to know."

"I do," I said, moving closer to her. "I want to know how it turned out. What you told me about Al has been haunting me. He's haunted this room every bit as much as Kim has. You said you liked his big feet. You said you loved everything about him. Holding his feet in the movies, and kissing his hair, and all the little presents he gave you, and the head rubbing and his mind and the yin and yang of rib eating. You made it all sound like a very great love. What happened?"

"It wouldn't be of any use to you. With what you've got in the play, you probably could still go after Meryl Streep or Valerie Bertinelli."

"Della, I need to know what happened."

"You won't be able to write about it."

"Please let me try to understand."

I moved from the bed onto the floor so I'd be nearer to her.

"I think you already lived a part of it all with Kim, but you're just like everyone else," she said. "Everyone forgets the downhill side of love. I should have let you write your requiem."

"What about the downhill side of love?" I reached up and held her hand.

She looked at me, and for the first time I felt she was beginning to trust me. "My downhill with Al started, I suppose, with his feet."

"What happened with his feet?"

"We had been together for over six months, and then one night came when we went to a revival movie house to see *Gone With the Wind*. I think that was the first time I remember that I didn't think I wanted to hold his feet anymore."

"You didn't like his feet then?"

"I didn't say I didn't like them. It's just that *Gone With the Wind* was the first movie we went to when I realized I had grown impartial toward his feet. They were like just plain feet."

"That's all they were to begin with."

"Yes, but somehow I had been tricked by nature or some force into thinking they were really something special. And that same week, I remember being in a sea cave with him at a beach, and I was going to lovingly kiss his golden hair. I recall looking at it that day and thinking, 'Oh, his hair really looks only like yellow kelp.'"

"Kelp?"

"Yes. Seaweed. I think I was first indifferent about his hair for a few days, but then I remember I didn't like his hair anymore. And I remember he made me walk miles along the seacoast so he could look in the windows of rich people's beach houses. I recall standing next to him and noticing that his brow line didn't look like a Greek god's anymore. The shape of his head looked more like something the archeologist Dr. Leakey would have unearthed on a dig."

"You were disappointed in the shape of his head?"

"David, it was all part of the changing, the downhill side of love. And the next month we stopped mutual grooming, the hand and the head rubbing got just forgotten about, all that gorilla stuff."

"That was a little peculiar anyway, don't you think?"

"Yes, but he stopped gushing over me too. Roses and chocolate-covered apricots were kaput."

"Nix with the gifts?"

"Yes. And I guess I got tired of his name-dropping, watching him running around the apartment house saying he'd just seen Sting, Tom Hanks, and Olivia Newton-John in the elevators. I began to think his mind wasn't so special at all either."

"What about him thinking he was a member of Mensa from another world?"

"That started to bother me. And I got to dislike his yin-and-yang approach to cuisine. He'd make up things like how all the members of Mensa bring only Hellmann's mayonnaise with them to restaurants because it's the only mayonnaise they'll use. And another time he yelled at me that I'd shown too much cleavage at a Wendy's—and I think I really knew it was going downhill when I had to watch him debone an entire chicken at Lola's Lucky Cluck Hot Barbecue Pit."

She eased onto the floor with me. She was

trembling and I held both of her hands trying to calm her. I knew she had to tell me everything if she was going to stand a chance—if *I* was going to stand a chance. "Did you ever think maybe you weren't getting tired of him, but that maybe your love was deepening in some way, or maturing?"

She tossed her head so her hair swung out of her eyes. "Yes, I considered that for about one second. But you know, by the end of another month I realized I hated his big feet."

"You hated them?"

"I really hated them. I began to notice that they knocked over furniture and knickknacks and they scraped wood floors. It got so I couldn't bear to see and hear them clumping around the house like Bigfoot."

"You could have overlooked them."

"Sure, but it wasn't only the feet I hated by now. I began to hate all of him."

"How did he feel about you?"

"Well, that was the other lesson I learned in life. *Never give your heart to a gusher.* Any boy who gushes over you can just turn it on easily and gush over any girl he meets."

"Did Al meet another girl?"

"Yes. He began to focus his gushing onto this one girl, a cheerleader from Manhattan High who had a body that didn't quit."

"What'd you do?"

"I started screaming at him, and he told me I had nothing to worry about, that the only reason he had to be nice to the cheerleader was because she was really his interplanetary Mensa squadron leader."

"He was really nuts."

"He began dating her and flaunting her right in front of me all the time."

"That's terrible."

"I began to hate myself. That's what happens, this is what it gets reduced to one way or another. I know couples where it sometimes takes them twenty years to get like that, where they were high school sweethearts, but it ends up that way anyway. Then came the last straw."

I put my arms around her and held her. "What was it?"

"Well, I began to see life for what it really is," she said. "It's one big singles cruise. All one class. Come in evening gown or shorts! And then one night I went to his apartment and I caught him making out with the cheerleader. They were making out like hyenas. And what does he do? He screams at *me*! And he told me he never wanted to see me again! Oh God, David," she suddenly said, "my baby daughter! My baby daughter!"

She burst into tears, but she didn't bury her face on my shoulder or turn away from me. The tears streamed out of her eyes and she kept looking at me. One glance into her beautiful, pained eyes and I became frightened, because I sensed something far more terrible than anything I had imagined had happened to her. Even I didn't want to think about it, but I knew it had to be said.

"You have something more to tell me."

"Oh David, he had promised me I'd live my whole life with him. That he'd love me forever in this world and all other worlds. He had promised me so much in the beginning, and I loved him so much, I did what he wanted."

"What did he want? What?"

"He made me give away my baby!" she sobbed. "My poor baby! He said it would be better for her, better for Tiara and me, that it was the only way he and I would have a chance for a life together! And I believed him! God, David, I believed him! And he made me go to an agency, and I signed the papers, and she was gone. My baby daughter was gone forever."

◆◆◆◆◆

Love is blind. . . .

—WILLIAM SHAKESPEARE

Della stopped crying. I got her a glass of orange juice from the kitchen. When I got back, she was standing out on the terrace. I put the glass in her hand, and she took a sip.

"When Al told me to get out of his life, I did just that. I took any books and papers I'd left around the apartment. I remember going to The Magic Bar in Chinatown. I knew the bartender. I drank margaritas for nine straight hours until I felt myself nearly dead. Then I had the bartender call me a cab. They took me to Bellevue for the first time. I thought I was going in the emergency-room entrance, but I made a wrong turn in the hallway. I had stumbled into the psychiatric wing by accident. But I met a nice doctor in the hall, a large distinguished guy in a white smock. He asked if he could help me."

A night breeze had come up. I put my arm around her, but she had her gaze fixed on the giant yellow moon. "I tried to tell the doctor, *'Yes, yes, I need help! I know what love is. I've got to warn everyone what love is or I'll die.'* But I was so stoned I couldn't get any words to come out. I was in a nightmare, where you yell and yell and nobody hears you—but finally I was able to say the name 'Al.' I said 'Al'—and I know this sounds crazy—but the only words I eventually could say were *'Al lets Della,'* and then I was able to say six words: 'Al lets Della' and 'Call Ed' plus the name 'Stella'—and I put them all together so I said *Al lets Della call Ed Stella*. I kept telling that to the doctor. And even in my stoned mind I realized I had stumbled into a palindrome—you know, one of those sentences that spell the same thing backward as forward! I thought I was brilliantly telling the doctor this message about love. That I had come up with a magic phrase for the doctor. *Al lets Della call Ed Stella*. I kept repeating it over and over, thinking he'd understand that my message for all teenage boys and girls everywhere, for everyone, was that love is born from terrible loneliness, and it always goes back to the same terrifying place! I thought I was telling the doctor about the face of love!"

"What'd he say?"

"Well, this was like love too. He moved closer to me, the doctor, and I felt he understood what I meant about love. I looked up into his eyes, and he looked into mine. It was like he was my father. My poor wonderful dead father! And then he lifted a silver whistle to his lips and began to blow it. Even his face of love changed, and his lips were inches from mine, only he was shouting *'Orderlies! Orderlies!'* And I tried to run away, but he was standing on my feet!"

"On your feet?"

"Yes. That's the way doctors are trained to detain you in a nuthouse! And the orderlies came and they took me away and locked me up in a padded cell, just like they did with Kim. And it took nine days for Actors Equity to spring me. After that, I just went home and stayed with my mother and became a regular drunk. Now I really have to leave, David. I'm sorry."

"You don't have to leave!" I said, putting my arms around her. "Don't you see that we both want the same thing! The real world's gone bonkers! We've got to make one ourselves. That's our play! And then I'll write another play! And another. And in between, we'll be able to roll with the punches. It'll be different with me, I swear! I love you."

"David, there's only one thing a writer really wants, and you should all have it chiseled on your gravestones: AT LAST A PLOT. You don't really love me. It just doesn't happen."

She broke out of my embrace, walked quickly through my room and headed down the hall. I ran after her. "Della, I do!"

"Good-bye, David Mahooley," she said, opening the door.

"Della, you can't pull a potato out of the ground to see if it's ready."

"What does that mean?"

"I don't know."

"David, you're not sensitive enough for me. Believe me, I've known enough boys to know. Call it my shortcoming, but if I was ever stupid enough to try to play the game again, it'd have to be with a guy who's sensitive. And you can keep my vodka," she added as she headed for the elevator.

Suddenly, I found myself screaming, *"I don't want you to leave! I've never been in love with anyone like you before! I'll never find anyone like you again! I'd love you even if you had two parrots on your head! You've touched my heart! You've touched my heart!"*

She pressed the elevator button. I ran back to my room and grabbed the biggest Caribbean drum. I took it and ran out of the apartment. Della saw me coming banging the drum as loud as I could. "I have passion!" I yelled. "I have it! Don't go! Please don't go! I've got a lot of passion! I've got it!"

The elevator door opened. She got in. The door closed. I spun around and ran back into my apartment, past my mother and father grinning on their camels, and out onto the terrace. I kept banging the drum. A really heavy mist was falling down from the hydroponic's terrace, and his dogs started barking. "STOP YAPPING! STOP IT! GAG THOSE MUTTS! GAG THEM, YOU VEGETABLE FREAK!" I was so whacked out, I put the drum down and ran to the refrigerator. I grabbed a carton of eggs my mom had left and raced back out onto the terrace. I hurled them up at the hydroponic's terrace, each one a splattering hit! I leaned over the railing. Below, I saw Della leaving the building. I shouted to her.

"DELLA! I HAVE PASSION! DELLA! LOOK AT ME UP HERE! DELLA! DELLA!"

But she turned onto Broadway and was gone.

I froze at the railing. I thought there was nothing that could happen to me to make me feel more miserable, but I was wrong. Suddenly a burst of hose water came shooting down from the phantom in his bathrobe. It caught me smack in the face and drove me back against the glass window like a moth. Water blasted into my nose and ears. It seemed to go on forever and thought I was going to drown!

Finally, the hosing stopped.

I picked up my wet drum and stumbled back into my room. I made it to the bathroom and began to dry myself off.

The intercom buzzed.

"What?"

"That wild girl's back," Joe said. "She's on her way up."

For a moment I thought he might be talking about Ed Weingarten.

I opened the front door. Della got off the elevator. She came toward me. My hair was still dripping.

"You're back."

"Yes," she said.

"The hydroponic hosed me. I'll go up there tomorrow disguised as a Cantonese Wok delivery boy, kick his big cucumbers, and teach those mean giant schnauzers to fly."

"No," she said, coming in and shutting the door. "He might be dangerous."

She went to the kitchen, grabbed some paper towels, and began to blot my head.

"Look, David, I don't know quite how to say this. I mean, I appreciated you saying you'd still love me if I had two parrots on my head. I only got a block down Broadway to the corner—where they have that Mud, Sweat, and Tears Pottery Shoppe and Personal Surveillance Equipment store and I got frightened . . ."

"Right by the newsstand?"

"Yes . . ."

"Did you see all those papers with headlines about killer cockroaches, cocaine-sniffing pigs, and that grandmother bride with her teenage groom?"

"No," she said, smiling, "but I thought about what you said—and all the crazy stuff you did on the terrace. Nobody ever showed *that* much emotion over me. I suppose what got to me most was the part where you said you really believed we could have something, David. Some kind of place for us, something of our own. I think I'd like to give it a try."

I sat down on the living-room rug.

"I'm glad. I'm very glad."

She brought in the whole roll of paper towels. "I was thinking maybe we could help each other, too. I mean, I wouldn't expect to be in every play you wrote," she said, "but I have lots of ideas, things I want to tell you about. I mean, I'm not a writer, but I did just think of something else that happened to me that might be good for your next play."

"What?"

"Well, there was this other boy I was seeing by the name of Johnny."

"Johnny who?"

"It doesn't matter. I didn't go out with him very long."

"Where'd you meet him?"

"At Bloomingdale's," she said, still patting me

dry. "I was looking at an eggbeater in the house-wares department, when this boy came over and stood next to me. He made believe he was looking at eggbeaters too, but then he whispered something shocking into my ear."

"What?"

"He whispered, *'Kill me.'* And then he repeated it. *'Kill me.'*"

"Oh, my God. What did you do?"

"You don't want to know."

"But I do," I said. "I really *do*. . . ."

◆◆◆◆◆
EPILOGUE
◆◆◆◆◆

It was fitting my parents were coming home on Halloween. That morning I got up, got dressed, and went to school. Mom and Dad would be landing at Kennedy Airport just after two P.M. and would be home by the time I got back. I had a lot to discuss with them, and I couldn't wait for them to meet Della. I thought maybe she could get dressed up again as the blind theater coach for the occasion.

The whole day at school was strange. There were more kids than other years running through the hallways with fake vampire teeth, rubber rats, and witch masks. Lunch had been a complete madhouse with kids biting fake-blood capsules and eating pizza slices with plastic Freddy Kreuger hands.

When the final bell rang I took my time collecting my books and getting my backpack together. Hordes of other kids rushed by me. A lot of the freshman were still into trick-or-treating and the juniors and seniors had been talking all day about going to a big school party at a rented hall on East Eighty-second Street. The tickets were really cheap. Della had plenty of costumes, and I could put together something with a blanket and plants and go as the Swamp Thing. It felt good to know at last I had a pal I could do things with.

Within minutes, I was pretty much alone in the first-floor hallway. A couple of teachers rushed to punch out at the time clock in the main office. Something made me stop in my tracks. At first I felt that I had lost or forgotten something, but I couldn't figure out what it was. I continued on as far as the stairs near the exit, but instead of going out of the building, I started up to the third floor.

The door to Mrs. Midgeley's classroom was open. I hadn't been in the room since Kim had tried to jump from the window. One of the cleaning men was emptying out the wastepaper basket into a canvas cart.

"Hi," he said.

"Hi." He looked like he knew I wanted to ask him a question. I got right to it. "Say, you wouldn't happen to know *which* window the girl tried to jump out of last term, would you?"

"Sure," he said. "That one there." He pointed to a half-open window at the back of the room.

"Thanks," I said.

"It's a shame," the cleaning man said. "She was a really pretty girl. Used to always say hello and give me a smile."

He moved on to clean the room across the hall and left me alone to check out the window. I went over to the wide wooden shelf that was the windowsill. A kid who had been in the class told me Kim had just suddenly climbed up onto a desk in the last row, then stepped over to the shelf and stood there looking out.

I opened the window. I saw the flagpole and, far below, the cement courtyard. I really hate high places because they do more than scare me. They draw me to them. It's like my mind short-circuits and says, "Hey, this is really high and I hate it. What if somebody pushes me, or suppose an alien takes control of my mind and *makes* me jump!"

I tried to feel what Kim must have felt standing there ready to leap. But I couldn't. Then the thought crossed my mind that probably I had never had a block at all. It was more like all along there had been something missing, an emptiness—not something standing in my way. All I could think of looking out the window was what it had been like not having a real friend. For me, for Kim, I guess for everybody on earth there's nothing worse than that.

I turned from the window and headed out of the room. I thought of Della coming into my life, as I started down the stairs. Whether our friendship lasted a month, a year, or a lifetime, I would never forget all that she had taught me.

I left the school knowing I had to see Della as soon as possible. I had a mind-boggling thought and I had to talk it over with her. Her instinct that the kid she met in Bloomingdale's near the eggbeaters would make a terrific next play for us to work on was right on the money. But I had come up with my own special touch. I could see the scene where the boy says, "Kill me, kill me." But *then* he meets my cannibal children who had invited their math teacher over for dinner, and they learn to *care* for each other! That really had dramatic possibilities.

It'd be great.

It'd be fantastic and original.

I just knew Della would love it.